D1277389

Withdrawn

ODE TO MY FIRST CAR

PRAISE FOR
A MILLION QUIET REVOLUTIONS

"Truthful, romantic, and compulsively readable, *A Million Quiet Revolutions* is filled with a million quiet revelations about living as your true self—whoever, wherever, and whenever you happen to be. I loved it."

—**DASHKA SLATER**, *NEW YORK TIMES* BESTSELLING AUTHOR OF *THE 57 BUS*

"Gow effortlessly reminds us that we queer people join a long lineage of historical queer people who might have dreamed of us as much as we dream of them."

—**ELIOT SCHREFER**, AUTHOR OF NATIONAL BOOK AWARD FINALISTS *ENDANGERED* AND *THREATENED*

"Told in achingly beautiful verse, Gow tells the story of two trans teens, both boys, as they struggle with identity and family and most of all, first love."

—**DONNA FREITAS**, AUTHOR OF *THE BIG QUESTIONS BOOK OF SEX & CONSENT*, *THE HEALER*, AND *THE NINE LIVES OF ROSE NAPOLITANO*

"Robin Gow's *A Million Quiet Revolutions* is a stunning, lyrical love story about discovering our identity (and what that means for us) and the importance of seeing ourselves reflected in history. A gorgeous debut."

—**NICOLE MELLEBY**, AUTHOR OF *HURRICANE SEASON* AND *IN THE ROLE OF BRIE HUTCHENS*

"An aching love letter to trans relationships that is equal parts nostalgic, raw, and hopeful."

—H.E. EDGMON, AUTHOR OF *THE WITCH KING*

"A beautifully written novel in verse about self-discovery and first love . . . A stunning YA debut."

— SCHOOL LIBRARY JOURNAL ONLINE, STARRED REVIEW

"Aaron and Oliver are frustrated that much of history ignores "what it was like to live as someone / other than a / white / Protestant / land-owning / man," and as they discover that life needn't follow gender binaries, their revelations ring with authenticity."

—BOOKPAGE, STARRED REVIEW

"A sweet and highly earnest transgender love story."

— KIRKUS REVIEWS

"Sweet details . . . and steadfast romance make for a compelling journey."

—PUBLISHERS WEEKLY

ALSO BY ROBIN GOW

A Million Quiet Revolutions

ROBIN GOW

ODE
TO MY
FIRST
CAR

Farrar Straus Giroux
New York

Farrar Straus Giroux Books for Young Readers
An imprint of Macmillan Publishing Group, LLC
120 Broadway, New York, NY 10271 • fiercereads.com

Our books may be purchased in bulk for promotional, educational, or
business use. Please contact your local bookseller or the Macmillan
Corporate and Premium Sales Department at (800) 221-7945 ext. 5442 or
by email at MacmillanSpecialMarkets@macmillan.com.

Library of Congress Cataloging-in-Publication Data is available.

First edition, 2023
Book design by Trisha Previte
Printed in the United States of America by Lakeside Book Company,
Harrisonburg, Virginia

ISBN 978-0-374-38843-0 (hardcover)
10 9 8 7 6 5 4 3 2 1

To my queer and trans community

Love shook my heart
Like the wind on the mountain
rushing over the oak trees.

—SAPPHO

ODE TO MY FIRST CAR

DAD SAYS,

"All first cars
have a way
of going out with a bang."
He picks me up
on the side of the road by the stoplight
near the Trappe Tavern.

My head is throbbing and I'm trying
to remember what happened
to you, my wonderful,
junky first car.

A policeman had asked me,
"Do you remember
your name?"

I said, "Yes . . . Claire Kemp.
I'm fine. I'm fine."

He was bald. He looked stern
as he asked, "What happened?
Have you been drinking?"

I thought to myself,
"You couldn't be nicer?
I just crashed my freaking car!"

I said, "No, of course not, it's like noon,
I was on the way
to visit my friend Sophia."

   My friend Sophia,
   who you'd carried with me
   on so many late-night drives
   on whirling backcountry roads
   and through the nearby forest. My friend Sophia

who I sometimes think I could drive away
with forever. My friend Sophia
who I (dear God) am pretty sure
I like as more than just a friend.
That's just how much she's been on my mind—
standing over the wreckage of you,
I'm somehow thinking about her.

The police officer jotted down
everything I said in a notebook,
        asking again, "What happened?"

"I think the gas pedal got stuck."

        "Mhm," he said.
        Was that him doubting me
        or just acknowledging what I said?

The car I rear-ended looked fine.
A big red van. The driver was
pretty angry. She was

huffing and pacing
on the sidewalk.

The officer went back to his car
and that was when

I first got a look at you, Lars. Your crumpled hood.
One headlight hanging off and lying
on the asphalt.
Next thing I knew,
the tow truck was there.

I asked, "Can you take it to Jim's repair shop?
That's where we go."

The tow-truck man furrowed his brow.
He bent down to look at the car.
"Honey, I don't think
it's gonna need a repair shop."

PART I

Odes to You, Lars

YOU, LARS

I only had a year with you, Lars,
but it felt like
so much longer.

I know it sounds dramatic
but my life didn't really start
until I started driving you—

those first times I didn't have to ask
for a ride to Sophia's house
or I could stay a little later
at band practice after school
because I wasn't waiting
for someone to pick me up.

I technically named you

but really you named yourself.
From the start, I always thought

you looked like a "Lars."
Sturdy
and tired.

Strong green but
not emerald green. Not showy.
A gentle and butch kind of car.

    Driving home with Dad I'm asking myself,
        "What the fuck am I going to do
        without you, without a car?"

    I keep thinking, "No no no no no—"
    I can't go back. I can't go back
    to Mom and Dad not trusting me—
        asking me every little detail of my plans—
        feeling always like I'm suffocating.
        They had just started to really let me

make decisions and go out on my own
and now that's all ruined. Beyond ruined.
There's no getting you back.

You were
my grandma Jean's car.

You were a lot like her.

She had short gray hair
and was always crouching in her garden
behind her tiny house in Oley, Pennsylvania.

When she gave you to me last year,
you still smelled like her cigarettes
and her pine air freshener still dangled
from the rearview mirror.

Now you are going
who knows where.

I wish we could have
one more drive.

I keep trying to go backward
thinking, "What if I didn't leave in a hurry . . .

What if my mind was more focused on the road . . .
What if I could do something
to change this?"

JUST LAST WEEK

I drove with you to get Panera with Sophia.
The Philly alternative radio station
came in all fuzzy and static but we left it playing anyway.

Sophia discovered that you had a moon roof and she said,
"Omg! Claire! There's a roof!!!
This is so cool!"

She reached up and opened it
and the bright noontime sun poured
across our faces. Even as the trees
blocked and unblocked light,
it still felt warm on our skin.

After we got food, we took the long way home.
      Sophia said, "We could go anywhere you know—
      we could like drive to the beach right now!"

"I think our parents would notice if we drove to the beach,"
I said, but I imagined it.

Us, in our shorts and T-shirts
parking you on the sand.

I keep thinking I wish we could have done it—
gone all the way to the beach.

Sophia is like that—always dreaming a new adventure.
I'm like—why didn't she convince me to go?

Now it's too late.
We won't get to do something like that, will we?

  Soon it'll be senior year
    and then graduation
      and then we'll both move away
        and then I'll have completely and totally

wasted my chances to tell Sophia
how I feel.

I KNOW

Most sixteen-year-olds don't get cars.
I blew my one shot to have one

and I
let you down.

There's no way
my parents would have ever gotten me a car.

Even when Grandma gave me the car,
they kept being like, "We have to think about it,"

when I asked to drive places
on my own.

They were still mad at me
for lying just that once.

Well, okay, it wasn't
just that once. They just caught me once.

I have lied a lot
but I do it because
if I don't lie,
my parents won't let me do like anything.

If they knew the whole truth—
they probably wouldn't even let me hang out with Sophia
        (which is basically the only thing they trust me to do).

So, when I was a freshman,
I lied about hanging out
with my ex-boyfriend (Liam).

I'd say I was going to band practice
or pit rehearsal and really, I'd just go to Liam's house.
When really, I'd quit band in the summer
because I hated band camp and honestly
I didn't even really like playing oboe that much.
I could never make it sound like anything
but a dying goose.

What makes me mad still is we didn't even really *do* anything.
Mostly I just hung out while he played video games.

I dated him because I thought having a boyfriend
made me like . . . I don't even know. It made me feel important?

Real? Like almost an adult? That and it felt like
everyone was getting boyfriends.

It was honestly
kind of cringe of me.

I was good at lying though!

Well, until one day Mom came early to pick me up
and there wasn't rehearsal at all because it was cancelled.

She came to an empty school parking lot.

The second my phone started vibrating next to me
on Liam's sofa, I knew she'd found out.

      I knew it was all over for me.

I KNEW IT WAS ALL OVER FOR ME

Lars, they didn't even know
I had a boyfriend!

Just figuring that out
would have gotten me in trouble.

I never thought of my family
as like super religious

until I started sixth grade
and I asked to go to the dance

and Dad made some comment
about dances not being appropriate for sixth graders.

They ended up letting me go
but they always made sure to point out

how I was different from other girls my age
because I didn't "show a lot of skin"

and I dressed "more modestly."
Ironic because I would say I actually dress a little "butch."

So basically, my parents are pretty open-minded
except when it comes to sex or sexuality.

Of course, that's like not something we've said aloud.
I don't even think I've heard them say, "sex"

but they talk around the subject.
Needless to say, I was officially grounded until the end of
freshman year.

The only good thing to come from it was
it made me break up with Liam which I wanted to do anyway.

The unofficial grounding lasted longer though.
I was only really allowed to see Sophia and a few other girls.

That was, until you came, Lars. It was like you arriving
opened them up to trusting me again.

SECRETS

I feel like you hold all the secrets
    and daydreams
    and meandering thoughts
        I had while I was driving you.

You were my own little home

in this middle-of-nowhere town
and outside of our freaking tiny apartment.

You gave me a place I could go
where I didn't have to hide
any part of myself,

unlike I have to with

my brother, Chris, my mom, and my dad.

ME: THE FAMILY'S LONE QUEER

It's complicated. I've always known I liked girls
but I didn't believe my own feelings
till the end of this last school year.

It's funny, Lars, I like kind of figured it out
just a little bit before I got you.

The specific moment
I knew
was on Sophia's couch (go figure).

It was almost midnight.
I drove you to that sleepover, remember?

It was the one
with all the girls from chorus and band (a lot of girls).

We were talking about
which movie we should watch

and Jenny was like,
    "What if we watched
    Blue is the Warmest Color?"
which everyone knows
is a BIG lesbian movie. Everyone laughed

but I felt like sad—I wanted to watch it???
Why did I want to watch THAT?

We ended up watching
Nick and Norah's Infinite Playlist and
I love that movie
but I was so annoyed the whole time

because all these girls who were my friends
just laughed at the "lesbian movie,"
so I didn't even enjoy it.

Why couldn't we watch a gay movie?

When I got home from the sleepover,
Blue is the Warmest Color was all I could think of

until I hunkered down
and watched the movie by myself. Earbuds in
and head down—
glancing to the door the whole time
in case someone walked in.

The sex scene
changed my life
but watching these two girls

kissing
touching
clutching each other

was so hard to do in my house. I had to sit
with my back against the wall
on my bed. I was so scared. Someone would catch me.

I wasn't sure
what Mom or Dad
would even say but I didn't want to find out.

I mean if they were mad I had a boyfriend,
what would they do about this?

They'd probably take my laptop
or like shut off the Wi-Fi for the whole apartment.

Even more, though, I was scared
that when I finished the movie there would be
no turning back.

Before then, I just always told myself
I just really, really cared about women—
I just really cared about the girls who are my friends

and it's true, I do! But there's also
something a little more. Even now, though,

sometimes I wonder if I'm actually queer.

I wish I could talk to my family about it.
I wish I could ask, "How do you know you like a girl?"
I wish I wasn't afraid to say, "I know I'm bisexual."
I wish I could talk to them about so many things right now.

AT SCHOOL

The only out queer person in my high school
is Steven,
two grades below me,
and he's gay.

I keep thinking,
we should be friends or something
but I think the only thing we'd have in common
is being queer

which isn't much to start a conversation.

What would I say??

"Hey, hear you're gay. I'm gay too!"
Then, I'd have to elaborate,
"Well, actually I'm bisexual
but sometimes I just say 'gay'
because it feels easier which is like
literally me bi-erasing myself."

Just like going by statistics
I know there must be other bisexuals here in Trappe,
but I feel super alone

especially because I can't drive off with you, Lars,
blasting Halsey or Janelle Monáe
or any of my other queer women and nonbinary icons
over your gritty speakers.

SUSPICIONS

When I first came out to myself,
I had huge suspicions about Sophia being bi
but now I kind of think
those were just wishful thinking.

Wouldn't she tell me by now?
We share just about everything.

Besides, she's trans and she told me that.
I feel like being bi would be easier than that, right?
I guess I shouldn't assume what that's like.

Sophia came out as trans when she was like six
and sometimes I try to think about
what that must have been like.

She doesn't talk about it a lot
because she says, "It was honestly so long ago—
like I don't remember being six, do you?
I just remember how happy I was
when Mom let me buy dresses the first time
and a huge, pink birthday cake."

Ugh, I wish I had her family sometimes—
they're so supportive of everything about her.

See! More evidence! If she wanted to come out as bi,
her family would also be totally cool with it, I'm sure.

They have trans flag buttons that say,
"You're safe with me," for God's sake.

But it's just hard to tell with girls who are
so bold and bubbly like her.

Like sometimes I'll be like . . . is she flirting?
when she'd touch my back lightly
or give me a playful / dramatic kiss on the cheek
to greet me when we go get coffee at Starbucks.

It's funny because her over-the-top-ness
is one of my favorite things about her
(she's a theater kid through and through)
but it's also the thing that's hardest to read.

Like, she doesn't treat other girls exactly like me
but she is always bright and inviting to everyone
and we are good friends. Girls sometimes touch
their friends in like a platonic way. Right? Right????

Also, if I tell her I'm bi, I'm like worried
she's going to instantly connect the dots
that I'm into her. Maybe that's a good thing?
But if she's not it's definitely a bad thing.

I'm worried things would be weird
and we'd like slowly drift apart.
Sometimes I think it would be better
to get to be her friend than to risk losing her.

OPPOSITES ATTRACT?

I usually hate the phrase "opposites attract"
because like not ALL opposites attract.
Like I couldn't date someone who thinks LGBTQ+ rights
don't matter—
that would be terrible.

But when it comes to Sophia and me—
it kind of does feel like that.

I prefer doing stuff like chorus where if I mess up,
I can just mouth the words. Like yeah, I try
and I do love music
but I hate the idea of like letting people down
or having people depend on me.

Sophia—she gets all the leads in the musicals.
Sure, she gets nervous too before shows but when she hits
her stride
she just blossoms on the stage.

She's never even taken dance lessons but still she moves
so naturally for the dance numbers.

Sometimes I'm like, why is she friends with boring old me
but then we'll have a quiet night in together
and I'll tell her that she absolutely needs to take a break for once.
Sophia is also involved in like every club possible at school.

I'll bring over face masks and a brownie mix for us to make
and she'll say, "Claire, I think I'd lose my mind without you
telling me to be like a person and relax once in a while."

When she says stuff like that I just—I just melt.
She makes me feel like I'm valuable for who I am
and that's not something I really feel like most places—
especially not with my parents and my brother.

SINGING IN THE RAIN

Last year our school put on *Singing in the Rain*
as the spring musical and Sophia was the lead,
Lina Lamont. I honestly don't like musicals that much
just because I'm not a break-out-into-song kind of person
but I went every night to see Sophia.

I watched as she twirled and sang,
falling in love with the character Don,
who was played by this senior guy
who had absolutely nothing on her.

The story itself was kind of boring until
I thought to myself, you know—the lead could be bisexual
and she's in a romance with a guy.

Heteronormativity isn't just that there's no stories
about same-gender love, but also that
everyone is like always assumed to be straight.
I liked the play more imagining Lina like that though,
to be honest, the musical was still pretty straight.

I brought a bouquet of different flowers to every show
and gave them to her at the end. On the last day of the show,
no one else who knew her came and she gave me a huge hug.

She said, "You're like the best friend in the world."

A little piece of me broke.
That word "friend" felt like
she was trying to say,
"We're just friends."

I said, "Nah, I don't want to miss seeing you."

She poked my arm, saying, "You hate musicals."

"I do but I can appreciate a lot of it."

She beamed and hugged me close.

And the hug felt like . . .
maybe she does *like* like me.

And literally every single interaction
is exactly like this.

Always a little evidence toward
her liking me back
and always a little against.

MY BROTHER AND I

We don't really talk much.

Since we started sharing a room,
we kind of just pretend the other person
doesn't exist.

Sometimes, when I think about it too much,
I get really annoyed that I don't really have
a room to myself anymore.

We make boring small talk on good days.

I used to play with my brother
all the time. We played "mountain men"
in the yard where we'd pretend to be
wilderness explorers or we'd be
astronauts on a new planet.

Now, we mostly just say "hello"
and "goodnight" and sometimes
"can you believe Mom said ____" or
"do you know when Dad will be home this week?"

Sometimes, I think I should try harder
to talk to Chris but I can't imagine
us having much in common.

He's a straight, nerdy, teenage boy.
He thinks playing sports, video games,
and listening to classic rock
is an ideal Friday night.

I'm a queer, directionless girl
who likes to take long walks by the creek
and listens to pop-punk.

What would we even talk about?

Sometimes I feel bad that I never offered
to really drive Chris that much.

I remember on one of those first nights
Mom and Dad let me drive you, Lars, to Sophia's,
    Chris asked, "Hey can I get a ride
    to Derek's house?"

I said, "Only if you're ready now."
I was in such a hurry. I guess I was
kind of an asshole for saying that.

    His face fell and he looked around.
    "Oh, I need a minute," he said.

"Well, I'm going," I said.
In the moment I felt
a twinge of guilt and I said,
"I'll take you next time."

He didn't ask again and I didn't offer.
God, what a dick I was.

I was just like so excited to get out.
Maybe that's also part of like why
we don't really click. It really is
kind of my fault.

I wish I could just go backward
and let me and him have that drive with you.

What could we have talked about?

What might Chris have told me?

What might I have told Chris?

ODE TO LEARNING HOW TO DRIVE

Lars, did I ever tell you
I learned to drive in my dad's jeep
in the church parking lot
and the winding cornfield roads?

When I first started learning,
I'd get so frustrated at myself
for not gliding smoothly

around turns—for needing
more and more practice.

Dad was always patient.
In a steady voice, he'd say,
    "Whoa, whoa hold on"
and
    "Claire! Check your mirrors"
and
    "Nice, very nice."

God, how could I fuck up this bad?
How did I crash you?
How did it happen so fast?

Every time I think about it,
a whole new level of guilt appears.

I keep thinking about how much money
a car is worth and how by crashing the car,
I basically just exploded a bunch of money.

Mom and Dad work so hard to save money—
to help us get by and my mistake just took so much away.
I'm thinking about it

and all the hours of work it would take
to buy a car. All those hours, gone.
I know it was free from Grandma, but
nothing is ever really free, right?

And Dad was always proud of
how quick I learned
and how dedicated I was to practicing.

He told me,
    "Claire, you're
    a natural driver."

        So much
            for that.

TRAPPED IN TRAPPE, PA

I might die of boredom
from being stuck here
ALL SUMMER.

I keep thinking about
how badly I wanted to drive
to the beach with Sophia
or offer to drive people into Philly for the day.

We're close-ish to Philly but the bus ride
to get there is
at least eighteen stops.

We're also close to Phoenixville
which is a very much less-crappy small town
but it's not close enough to walk

and the bus only comes
twice a day. Same thing
with the huge King of Prussia Mall.

Do you remember driving to all those places?

I remember the traffic into Philly
for that Panic! At the Disco concert
and trying to parallel park like 8,000 times
on Bridge Street in Phoenixville and losing you
in the mall's huge parking lot.

I swear, it's almost like
they want to keep you trapped in Trappe
which is just barely a town at all.

All the towns around here
are just a block or two–sized, like why not

just lump them all together? I guess the real problem is
I have a whole summer before school starts again
and nothing to do without a car.

If I'm being honest,
which I know I can be with you, Lars,
I'm also upset because there's nowhere
to make out without a car.

I keep thinking
even if Sophia likes me too,
where would I invite her?

Sure, we could go to her house
and her parents would probably
not mind us dating
but it wouldn't be the same as like
driving to the woods
and parking.

Sitting on your hood
and staring up at the wild bright stars
between kisses.

Ugh. Have to stop torturing myself.

Where am I going to go now?

Behind the giant supermarket? (Kidding, that's gross.)
Behind a dilapidated house? (No, sir, I'm not getting haunted.)

I guess that's getting ahead of things anyway.
I'm not dating Sophia—
I'm not dating anyone
or even "talking" to anyone—

unless you count Sophia,
who I text all day and night
and morning, which doesn't make the
trying-not-to-obsess over her any easier
but no, she doesn't count
because she's just my best friend.

She doesn't have a car either
and I'm not going to ask Mom
to drive us somewhere—
I'm like sixteen!

I just wish I could grow up a little faster.

I wish I graduated this year
but I have a whole year more of school in this place.

I feel like I'm not going anywhere.
Like time has completely STOPPED.

DO I HAVE MY PHONE?

Shit! And I have to text Sophia to tell her
I crashed my car, she's probably
still waiting for me to come.

Thank GOD I do have my phone. I take it out
and think for way too long
about how to word the text

so it's not too freaking alarming.
It's not every day someone texts you,

"I just crashed my car!"

I HAVE LIKED SOPHIA SINCE BEFORE I KNEW I LIKED GIRLS

Maybe you, Lars, noticed before I did,
when I'd drive her home after school

and let her pick the radio station and glance over
as she opened your window just a crack

to let the wind whip her long, curly brown hair
in all directions. We weren't friends in elementary school

but I used to notice the way she would wear her hair
in three wonky ponytails.

In my room, I tried putting mine up like
that but it never looked as cool.

I didn't always have this crazy a crush on her.
It's been kind of a slow burn. It felt like everything

was leading up to this summer—our summer of love.
Then, everything happened to you, Lars, and it was over.

In middle school, Sophia and I started to talk more because
she was in my art class. We sat next to each other.

She hung out with the more artsy people
and I hung out with the anime geeks.

These two groups of people do have some overlap.
Still, slightly different friend groups.

I sucked at art though and dreaded going to class.
I preferred just reading manga and romances.

I'd look over and see her bright, beautiful flower pastels
and her watercolors of golden-leaved autumn trees.

It's not that I didn't like doing it,
I just knew nothing I made would come out all that great.

Even now, I am still drawing lollipop trees
and round suns with little pointy rays.

I think I'm pretty good at science
and I used to be good at math but ever since Algebra III,

I've felt like I might be less good at math.
Sophia is somehow good at everything.

I love her brain and the way she finds
connections in everything. One day after school

when we were walking to chorus practice she said,
"I've been thinking art and math

are more related than people think.
Like, I measure lines on my sketches of animals

to get the right proportions. I wish we didn't teach things
so separately." That totally blew my mind.

It also explained why her drawings are always so precise:

cow drawings that look like
black-and-white photographs—dog doodles

that look like snapshots.

"CLAIRE? CLAIRE. HELLO?"

I blink. I forget I'm in Dad's jeep
still driving away from our wreck.

"What?"
            "Were you listening at all?" Dad asks.

"I'm sorry I got distracted.
I had to text Sophia that I wasn't going to meet her."
"You were just in a car crash and you're texting?"

"I'm sorry.
I just wanted to let her know.
I didn't want to leave her waiting."

I feel so stupid
and embarrassed.
"Claire . . . please tell me you at least had the brains
to not be texting and driving when this happened."

Dad's voice is short and tight.
He's talking like a clenched fist.

"Come on, Dad, I only do that at stoplights . . ."
Stern silence

"Kidding! I'm kidding.
I know not to.
I'm sorry I shouldn't kid right now."
"No you shouldn't," he says.
He pinches the bridge of his nose.
I can't tell if he wants to scream
or cry
or both.

FAREWELL

We drive to the shop where the tow truck took you, Lars.

I'm sobbing by the time we get there and I don't know why.

I mean, of course I know why, but you're just
a car. This is not that big a deal.

I guess I just am realizing how much you gave me

and how I fucked it up. I'm in this

my fault
  my fault
    my fault spiral.

Dad's talking to the mechanic
and I'm not saying anything.

They're laughing now
and talking about something or another.

I check my phone and Sophia hasn't texted me back.

I'm telling myself there's no way she *like* likes me
and we'll probably always be just friends.

Why would she like someone
who fucks up as much as me?

Then the nicer voice comes in
and says I'm being too hard on myself—
that I'm being mean to myself for no reason.

I didn't mean to do anything wrong.

Dad is talking to me but I'm not sure what he's saying.
He snaps his fingers.

        "Claire? Are you all right? Does your head hurt?"

"A little but I'm just kind of still taking it in."

        The mechanic walks away.

        "I'm sorry honey, but they say they have to scrap it."

"What?"
        "They can't fix the car.
        I'm sorry, Claire, we just have to scrap it."

He doesn't sound that sorry.
He sounds upset—again like he might cry.

I nod. I think deep down I knew
there was no fixing you
the moment I saw your crunched hood.

"Okay. Can you drive me to Sophia's?"

Why is that what I say?

I don't know. I'm ridiculous.
I regret it the moment I say it.

"God—Claire why???" I think.

> Dad sighs.
> "We should go home."

"I'm sorry that was stupid—
I shouldn't have said that."

> Dad doesn't reply, just starts
> walking back to the jeep.

I want to ask him to stop
and let me say bye to you
but he'd think
that was ridiculous.

So farewell, Lars.

Just this morning
you were parked on the side of the road
by our apartment. Just this morning

the sun glinted dully
off your scuffed green doors.

DRIVING HOME

I get more and more anxious that Sophia
hasn't texted me back.

I'm terrible about this. Whenever anyone
takes like more than thirty seconds to respond,

I'm always like, "Whelp they hate me."
It's a bad habit—especially because I KNOW

sometimes I don't even respond right away.
I wish I could throw my phone out the jeep's window.

"Are you sure you don't want
to drop me off at Sophia's?" I ask Dad.

> He's quiet too long and finally says,
> "You should be home."

"But I'll get even more upset."

> After another uncomfortable silence he asks,
> "Who will drive you home?"

"Maybe Sophia."

> "Does she have a car?"

"Hmmm . . . maybe. Maybe her mom does . . .
You could just take me there
and I can figure it out,
I promise."

I want to do ANYTHING
but go back home to deal with what
Mom and Chris and Dad
will say about me crashing you, Lars.

> "Okay," he says blankly.

> "We'll have to talk more later.
> I agree. Maybe you need a moment to think about it."

> I hope he doesn't tell Mom
> > but of course, he's going to.

Oh Lars, I'm sorry
and I miss you already.

MOM AND DAD AND CHRIS AND ME

So, like I said, we live in a tiny apartment right now.
I miss our old apartment on Main Street
where we each had our own room. We were on

the first floor and there was a sliding glass door
that led to a backyard we shared with
the upstairs neighbors.

Chris and I grew up in that apartment
and there were still red crayon marks on the backs of doors
from when we were little and creatively destructive.

I mean I knew it wasn't "ours"
because we rented it
but it always felt like it belonged to us.

We just moved this year
since Mom got her hours cut at the salon
and Dad's job stopped offering overtime.

None of it is fair.

Mom works hard
but the salon still wanted to make room
for some of the younger stylists
who get haircuts done quicker
and have more clients coming in.

I guess it made me realize
it doesn't always matter if you're
a hard worker, sometimes
the world is still crappy to you.
When I think about it too much,
I start just feeling like
what's the point of anything, you know?

But then I think about all the things I love
like walking in nature

and singing alone to myself
whenever I find the chance.

Those things are amazing
and then I think the world is actually pretty awesome,
it's just work that sucks.

In my bedroom in the old place, I'd eavesdrop
on Mom and Dad trying to figure out
what to do. I didn't sleep well. I daydreamed

about winning the lottery or something
for them—so that everything could go back
to normal. I just wanted to help. I still do.

This apartment is way too small.
and way too tight. There's barely enough space
to even do homework. Half the time

Chris's and my worksheets would get shuffled together
from working next to each other at the kitchen table
while Mom was always bumping into our chairs

as she tried to make dinner
on the tiny two-burner stove.

It's just not fair.

You know, Lars, I always tried
to stay out of here as much as possible.

Now it's going to be a lot harder without you.

I keep wondering like
if you were a person, what would you say to me?

Would you be disappointed in me too?

At least Dad is a truck driver so he's gone
for a few nights every week.
Still, those nights always feel empty.

How many times can I contradict myself?

Like I said, I share a room with Chris.

We've both never acknowledged how much we hate it.

How the hell
could I even invite someone over?

Where would we even go?

WHAT I WANT

Maybe it's the microscopic apartment
and I don't want to sound like weird or anything
but this summer I really want to have sex with someone.

I know that sounds really direct. It's just something
I've been thinking about. I've never done anything
with anyone at all. I don't even know

if there's any other queer people in Trappe
but I think it's worth a shot.
Is that bad? I think the whole concept of

"losing your virginity" is like gross.
I'd still also really like
to have my "sexual debut" already.

I'm 100 percent sure I'm bi so it's not like I want to test that—
but I always imagined I'd like experience something by now.

Plus, I think if I sleep with someone, anyone
it also might like get my mind off the Sophia stuff.

Is that a bad reason to want to have sex?

I think about the girls in *Blue is the Warmest Color*.
Adèle is like sixteen when she meets Emma.
Where is my Emma? An artsy girl

to like whisk me away . . . gosh that's ridiculous.

Yes, I know I said I like Sophia,
I guess I just always tell myself

that's not possible.
That's just something I'm supposed to
keep inside until it finally goes away.

Maybe I'm just confused.
No, I'm not confused,
curse you internalized bi-phobia.

I mean I guess it doesn't have to be a girl.
I still like guys
and I still like nonbinary people.

But, anyway, I shouldn't worry too much because
the odds are against me having sex
with anyone considering
my house is a miniature mess
and my family is all over the place
and they're going to be
stricter than ever
because of this accident.

I'm trying to like find some positives.

I think I did get lucky.
At least Chris isn't too loud and at least

Dad only yells at the TV when there's football games on
and at least Mom is sometimes in a good mood
and we sometimes all bake together in the small kitchen.

Last weekend we made
those pre-packaged cinnamon buns
and they were so, so good and the white icing dripped
everywhere.

Do you understand what I mean when I say
I want to spend more time with my family
and also never be around them at all?

I like them. I do. I just also wish I had
my own space.
That space was you, Lars.

I'm such an idiot.

I can't believe
I crashed you.
How did I do that? Did the gas pedal
really get stuck or am I just saying that?

The worst part about the accident
is I trust myself even less
than I did before.

I thought I was doing so good—
making Mom and Dad proud.

Keeping everything about me that's messy
out of sight—

and then, all this.

ODE TO THIS SUMMER

I have been thinking about "odes."

This past year in school
we learned about all kinds of poetry,

but I liked the idea of an ode best.

An "ode" is basically a poem dedicated to
or spoken to something or someone.

I think all my poems are odes. Here's one for you:

O Lars.

O Lars. I miss the clanging sound you made
when I started you up early in the morning.

I miss drives to nowhere and the cracks
in your seats. I miss the faint smell of pine

from the far-too-old air freshener—the tiny 2D pine tree.
Lying in your back seat in the parking lot

of a grocery store or strip mall.
I will miss most that feeling of

not having to be headed anywhere. I could
just exist with you somewhere far enough

away from home to feel briefly free—
like floating on a raft drifting away from land.

SLEEPOVER

I can't believe I'm crying about you again.
I'm lying on the floor in Sophia's bedroom.

    "I never had a car
    but I'd cry too if I broke my car,"
    Sophia says.

"I don't even know what I'm crying about—
no maybe I do—I had so many plans of what I wanted
to do with Lars."
That's what I say
but really I wanted to say,
"There's so many things
I wanted to do with you, Sophia."
I did want to do stuff with you, Lars,
but you understand, right?

Sophia lays down next to me.
My heartbeat quickens.
"You want to tell me about them?"

"What?"

"The plans, silly. What you wanted to do."

Sophia is like the best person to be around
when you're upset.

She has this way of making you feel like it's safe
to say anything. She doesn't instantly try
to make you feel better when you're sad,
she like makes space to talk about it.

I always feel bad though because
she'll almost never open up
when she's feeling down.

Like, when her dog died a few months ago
she literally didn't tell me
till I came over to visit and I was like,
"Where's Noodle?" and she finally told me.

She said she didn't want me to feel sad
and I was like—it's okay if I feel sad—
I want to be there for you.

"Okay so you can't judge me," I say, sitting up.

"Okay?"

I realize that mostly
I wanted to sleep with Sophia in my old car
but I obviously CAN'T say that so I say,
"I kind of wanted to hook up with people
in my car."

Sophia laughs.
"Are you crying about not getting to
have sex in your car?"

"I had it all year and
I never did that not even once."
I'm smiling now
because it is pretty funny.

"Who would you fuck?"

I try to remain calm and not blush.
I try to think of anyone—anyone at all
who it might make sense for me to like.
"Dani . . . maybe."

"Haha, I knew you liked him."

"Yeahhh," I lie.

"He is hot. Idk he's a little too nerdy for me."

"What about you?"

"Me?" Sophia asks.

"Yeah—if you could hook up with someone in a car."

"Why specifically in a car?"

"That's what we're talking about."

Sophia ponders this a moment. "Chris."

"Ew, Chris?" I say.
I guess it was a long shot
but I was hoping she'd say a girl—
even if it wasn't me.

"That's my answer."

"You've never—right?"

"No not ever."

"Me either," I say and I hate how even close friends
talk around sex. Not about it.

Sophia smiles mischievously.
Which I know means
she has an idea.

"What?" I ask,
getting excited.

A TERRIBLE IDEA

"Tell me!" I plead.

"No no no—it's too much."

"Come on please,"
I say and because she won't tell me
I'm like . . . what if she wants
to hook up with me?

Then I'm like, no Claire,
that's not what she's thinking.

"You're going to think I'm a slut."

"What's wrong with being
a slut?" I ask.

"True."

"Sophia, we should celebrate sluts.
I just admitted to you
that I'm sad about crashing my car
partially because now, I can't have sex in it."

She finally says, "Okay all right, are you ready?"

"Yes PLEASE.
I'm dying."

"What if we try to hook up with people this summer
but we have to try to hook up in cars."

"What do you mean?"

Sophia waves her hand. "You're right it's dumb."

"No, go on."

"What if we like try to think of all our crushes . . .
especially our crushes with cars, of course . . .
and see if they want to hook up this summer?
In honor of Lars . . . of course."

"Of course," I tease.

"See, I was right
you do think it's dumb."

"I just think car sex is spontaneous—
you can't plan for it."

I'm trying to accept
that Sophia didn't want to confess
her love for me.

"Well, we can try. I mean why not? It might help us
put ourselves out there."

I'm a little nervous but I say,
"Okay yeah sure it does sound like fun.
What's the plan?"

Sophia jumps up to grab her notebook from her desk.
"I'm glad you asked!"

ODE TO OUR FIRST DRIVE ALONE

After I got you, it still took me a few weeks to convince
my parents
I could actually drive alone.

Partially because of the incident with Liam but also because
I'm the first kid to do everything. Maybe also a little bit because
I'm a girl.

I swear they're more chill with Chris
and he's literally three years younger!

Anyway, they finally agreed because
it was only a short trip to King of Prussia Mall.

What I didn't realize was people drive RIDICULOUS
around there and the parking lot was a nightmare.

I drove around trying to park for like
literally an hour and a half before I just parked super far away.

Even though it was nerve-racking I felt somehow
free—like I was finally grown-up. Like if I wanted to, I could
drive

anywhere. To another state. Into Philadelphia or another city
entirely.
It made me feel like I wasn't anchored to this town.

Before driving home, I took a moment to just lay down
in my back seat and look up through the moon roof—

it looked like a television showing only the sky.
I watched the blank blue fill with cloud.

WHAT I *REALLY* WANT

"This summer we're going to be
big and bold and do what we want,"
Sophia says proudly.

In the back of my head
I'm like . . . if my parents don't
lock me in my room
but I say, "I want that so much."

She riffles through her desk
for a notepad, proclaiming,
"We're going to say what we want and
how we feel."

I admit, "To be honest,
I think I needed the added challenge
of trying to have sex in a car
to make me
willing to put myself out there,
you know?"

"Totally," she agrees.

"I'm about to be a senior in high school
and I've only ever kissed one person,"
I say.

"Ew and it was Liam,"
Sophia says.

"Not that there's anything
wrong with that—but I WANT to kiss people—
I WANT to do more with people. I'm just too shy
to ever say so," I say,

and it's so ironic I'm literally saying this to Sophia—
the person who I actually am not telling
exactly how I feel.

I am a hot mess, aren't I, Lars?

The thing about relationships,
whether you want to be friends or date or just hook up,
is that you have to say how you feel.
You have to be direct.

I'm basically the worst person
at that ever.

THE PLAN

Sophia finally finds her notebook
to write down lists of people we want to
get with this summer.

I don't really want to hear all the people
she likes but the moment is exciting so I push through.

Sophia draws it out like a chart and we
go back and forth till we each have four names written down.

"Four is a reasonable number for the summer . . . right?"

"Totally," I say,
and I'm thinking . . .
"FOUR people??? How am I
supposed to find four people
I even like enough to sleep with?"

"Aim low, right?"

"Yeah," I say,
also realizing
I'm basically encouraging Sophia
to sleep with people
who aren't me!!!

"You go first," I say.

"Theo."

"Damn I was going to say Theo . . . Can I add him too?"

"Of course!"

"Pen."

"Ryan."

"Daven."

"Allen."

"Maddy."

"Hmm . . . gotta make the last one count . . .
Let's say 'Simon.'"

CLAIRE	SOPHIA
Theo	*Theo*
Pen	*Ryan*
Daven	*Allen*
Maddy	*Simon*

COMING OUT (SORT OF)

Sophia nods. "This is great."
She looks up at me and there's this long silence
before she says, "Can I ask you something?"

Which you can't really say "no" to so
I of course say "Yeah."

"Are you like bisexual now?"

When she says it the word sounds almost clinical.

Shouldn't she know this? Shouldn't this feel
like more of a celebration?

When she told me she was trans
I was like happy—happy she trusted me
and proud of her. Why doesn't it feel the same right now?

I mean I send her
LGBTQ + TikToks all the time—
she shouldn't look so surprised.

I guess I never Came Out
but I thought Sophia knew on like some level
because we talk about LGBTQ + issues sometimes
and I'm always so fiercely pro-queer.

If she were bi, would she say it like that?

I guess maybe she's worried
because she's realizing it could mean
I have a crush on her.

"Yeah I'm bi I think."
Why did I add "I think"?
Damn it, Claire—be firm about something.
I exhaust myself, Lars, I really do.

    Sophia nods. "Cool.
        You think?"

"Still figuring out if I like guys."
I pause.

There's an awkward silence.

"And . . . you?" I ask
and I can't believe I worked up
the courage to say this.

    Sophia pauses.
    "I mean you see I picked guys."

"Doesn't mean you couldn't be . . .
something else," I say.

Sophia seems like she's thinking
but I can't read the look on her face.

Is she upset???

Is she upset at me for asking???

    "Yeah I think I don't know yet."

"Oh cool," I say.
Cool? Cool? I never say "cool."

Now she has to know
I have a crush on her.
Oh God I'm like ruining everything tonight.

    "Is that okay?" she asks
    with a little sharpness in her voice.

"Oh my gosh Sophia of course.
I didn't mean
to like put you on the spot."

    "I didn't know you were bi.
    Are you out?" she asks.

"I don't really want to come out.
I don't know it doesn't seem necessary," I lie.

I lie even though
I just promised myself
I'd be more honest from now on.

    Sophia nods again.
    "I'm sorry I never asked, I just thought
    you were a really great ally or whatever.
    That's me having main character syndrome I guess."

I laugh and that disperses the tension a little.

I want to ask Sophia more
like, "Do you consider yourself queer?
Questioning? Another label?"

I don't want to make her uncomfortable though.

Maybe she just doesn't want
a label at all.

BISEXUAL

Sometimes being bi feels like
I'm both pretending to be gay
and pretending to be straight.

At first this feeling made me think
I was just making it all up
but now I think about it as a queer feeling—

that in-between excitement.
I wish there were more queer people
at my high school. I want to tell

someone else about this feeling.
Lars, you're now my queer confidant.
Are you bi? No, I bet you just

prefer "queer" to describe yourself
considering cars don't have sex / romantic lives.
I really need to make more queer friends . . .

Anyway! I picked girls on my list because
Pen and Maddy have given me the feeling
they might be queer too.

It's pretty much a universal truth that
girls with undercuts are some type of queer.
We'll see, and whether they are or aren't,

they might still not be like into me
even if they are queer. It's so complicated.
I think straight people think that

queer people are just all into each other.
I wish it were that easy. We're just as particular
but with a smaller dating pool. I've never considered

coming out to my parents after everything with Liam.
Not chancing that kind of reaction again.
It's just safer to get through high school

and then start my life when I graduate. Plus,
they have enough to deal with. Dad works long hours
and Mom is always picking up odd jobs

to help us get by.
It doesn't seem necessary to make them
deal with learning all about queer stuff too.

Also, I'm scared if I came out and had to go through all that
and then ended up with a guy, they'd think I was lying,
or they just wouldn't get it at all.

Lars, is it really so hard
to understand?

I DON'T WANT TO TALK ABOUT IT

Like we usually do,
Sophia and I crawl up onto her couch
and watch *The Great British Baking Show*.

We're almost out of seasons but we pretend
that the show will keep going forever.

We play episode after episode.

It's late when she asks me,
"What was the car crash like?
How bad was it?"

I flinch.
I feel this tingling sensation all over.

I'm overwhelmed by the feeling that
    I never want to talk about it ever again.
        I've never felt like this before and I try
            to just shake it off.

I'm thinking about my head   smacking
                    the steering wheel —
                                my ears ringing.

    "Hey are you okay?" Sophia asks.

I blink. Yes. Yes, I am okay, I tell myself.
"Yeah, just zoned out."

    "Yeah, you did have quite a day."

"It was bad.
I don't think
I want to talk about it."

    Sophia nods. "That's totally fine.
    I get it.
    I'm sorry that happened."

She pets my hair
and it calms me down.

STAYING UP LATE

It's funny how the older you get, the less exciting
staying up late is.

Sophia and I are bored of watching Netflix.
I ask if I can just stay the night.

I don't want to go home and have my parents
talk about the crash. I'm kind of just trying

to pretend it didn't happen and that
you're parked in Sophia's driveway, Lars.

It wasn't that big a deal. I don't know why I'm
making such a big deal about it. It's not like

anyone was hurt. It's not like
we even paid for you, Lars. That doesn't mean

you weren't important but

why do I feel so shaken up by all this?
If I start thinking

about all those afternoons we went on drives,
I start to tear up. If I start to think about the crash,

I get dizzy. I just want to stay with Sophia
where I'm safe and I have someone who understands.

And, when I stop thinking about it long enough,
I can pretend it's just another Friday night in June.

I'm going to have to survive like at least all year
without a car.

> "You wanna do something?" Sophia asks,
> flicking off the TV.

"At eleven?"

> "Yeah why not.
> Let's like walk to Wawa."

CURFEW

I think curfews are a rumor. Maybe they existed once
but I've never heard of a high schooler actually being told
to go home for being out too late. Still, it makes

Sophia and I nervous as we walk to Wawa in the dark.
We use our phone flashlights even though
suburbia is nowhere near dark even this late.

We pass the college campus where, during the school year,
we always hear music thumping from a few houses on Main
Street.
Everyone at high school talks about going to

college parties but I think they all make it up.
I wish everyone wasn't always obsessed with
being older than they are. I feel this pressure to

want to be eighteen and sure I want to move out
and sure, I wish I had you, Lars, to escape with
but being seventeen isn't the worst I guess.

Haha . . . I mean yeah it kinda is the worst but
I also do love just walking with Sophia and talking
about nothing—how the streetlights make her face

look brilliant and glowing—how I can faintly imagine
what I'll get at Wawa and know that there's
a little bit more time to figure out what the hell

I'm going to be
and what I'm going to do
when I graduate in a little less than a year.

NEXT YEAR

Sometimes I'm jealous that Sophia knows
exactly what she's doing after high school.

> Actually, Sophia has known what she wanted to be
> since middle school: a music teacher.

There was a little bit of time where
I wanted to be a teacher too but mostly just because

> it was nice to have something to bond with Sophia over.
> (I could never be a teacher—hordes of children and stress
> are not my strengths.)

Well, I guess that's not entirely true.
I kind of think I'm bad at everything when really

I'm like OKAY at everything which is almost worse
than being bad. Before the teacher thing

I used to want to be a hairdresser like my mom
but she said she wants me to go to college

and do something "better than her."
There's honestly nothing that seems more fun

than doing hair or makeup and talking
to people all day. I have this dream

of starting a full salon just for LGBTQ+ people
so everyone would feel comfortable

experimenting with different looks.
I don't know. I know that's kind of a fantasy.

I keep telling people I might try to go
for art or design because I do like photography

and I'm taking a class this year on Photoshop.
So maybe I'll like that? Who knows?

It's so scary to have to like think about the rest of my life
all the time. It makes it hard to like enjoy stuff.

Like, I'll be having fun on Photoshop
and a thought will pop into my head like,

"Do you like this enough to make it your whole career?"
Fuck if I know, right?

WALKING BACK

As we walk back, Sophia talks about
all the colleges she's visiting this month.

I try to listen but they all kind of just
wash over me. I've been thinking of

maybe going to school in Philly because
it's close by and not too scary.

I say, "I wish I knew what I wanted to do
like you do."

Sophia says, "I wish I understood myself
like you do."

"What do you mean?"

"You know what you like
and what you don't like.
I just try to do good at everything.
It makes it hard to like know
what I actually like to do."

"I'm not sure if that's true.
Haha, if anything,
I feel even more directionless
than ever—half the time
I change my mind
halfway through a sentence.
Whenever I meet with the guidance counselor,
I just try to make something up
that sounds good."

"Really? Well that makes me feel
a little better."

"It's cool you're bisexual.
I kind of wish I had a label
that really feels like it fits me sometimes."

"I get that.
What about GENIUS?"

"Haha no—you know what I mean, stupid!
I mean for my sexuality."

"What about STUNNING?"

"Stop it, Claire," she laughs,
shoving me playfully.

I check my phone and I have a text
from Mom which is never a good sign

because she calls when it's good news
and texts when it's bad.

I stop walking for a second.

MOM: u crashed ur car and u go to ur friend's house right after?
lots to talk about Claire! what were you doing? that car was ur
grandma's! she worked so hard so u could have this one nice
thing

MOM: i'm sorry i'm just worried. u could have gotten hurt.

MOM: we will be talking

FALLING ASLEEP

When I stay over at Sophia's, I sleep on the floor.
She always offers for me to sleep in bed with her
but even before I told her I'm bi that felt a little weird.
I'm glad she still says it though. It makes me feel like
she doesn't see me any differently.

As I fall asleep, I think about all the naps I used to take
in my car. I think about how I'd planned to
take another nap this Sunday in the parking lot
of church. I've been skipping for a while by just

going to a different mass than my mom and
by "going to a different mass" I mean not going

to mass and, again, sleeping in the parking lot.
I know that seems really bad but honestly

I felt like it was kind of religious somehow—
like by lying close to church I was almost going.
Naps are spiritual when you're inside your own car.
It's like you have your own world even if only
for an hour or so.

A GUIDE FOR NOT GETTING IN MORE TROUBLE WHEN YOU'RE SEVENTEEN AND OVER IT

1.
Don't argue at all with your parents.
Just listen. Tell them you're so sorry,
even if you're not. You might feel
kind of bad. Just sit through whatever
they have to say.

2.
You can zone out a little bit but you
have to remember a few things
they say so that you can reply
in an effective way. For example,
"I know a car accident is serious"
and "I apologize for going over Sophia's
afterwards. I should have taken
more responsibility."

3.
They will probably issue
a punishment after this exchange.
Take said punishment. You know
your parents and you know they'll
let up on it. Don't gasp or groan

even when they say,
"You're grounded for
the next four weeks
at least."

4.

Cry and apologize more.
No matter how old you get,
crying is always effective.

5.

Do not go to your room.
Sit and cry in an open space
so that your parents feel worse.

6.

When your parents offer to reduce
your sentence, tell them you're
willing to last the whole month
and when they call you out
on your bullshit, just tell them
you're being sincere.

7.

Congratulate yourself
on lessening your grounding
from one month to one week.

8.

Resist the urge to brag to
your brother about your skills.

EXECUTING THE PLAN

How does anyone learn how to flirt?
I have, of course, watched movies
and TV shows and read scenes in books
but does it ever ACTUALLY happen like that?

It always seems like such a game.
It seems like really tiresome.

All throughout my grounding,
Sophia and I texted about our plan—
where and how we might be able
to meet up with people on our lists.

It actually made the grounding worse
because not only was I not allowed to see her
but I was also hearing about all her plans
to meet up with other people.

Yes, I created my own little personal hell.

To really put the nail in the coffin
Sophia texts me today, the last day of my grounding,
to say this:

SOPHIA: Would you believe me if I told you
Theo and I are texting?!?!

I set the phone down and walk to the bathroom
to splash water in my face, bumping past Chris
on the way.

I'm thinking ALREADY? You're ALREADY
talking to him? How did she do that?
I haven't even reached out
to anyone I wrote down.

To be fair, Theo and Sophia are already
kind of friends. You know like when you have
tangential friends who you somehow have
their number but you never text? But still.

Sophia is kind of friendly with everyone.
I guess I knew she'd have an easier time with this.
And, I'm trying to look at bright sides—

I do know she's at least thinking about her sexuality.
That's better than her just being like
"Nope, I'm 100 percent straight."

TEXTING

I know when people say "texting" they mean
flirty texting. She sends me screenshots
and somehow, some way, she manages
to make mundane questions kind of like sexy or whatever.

SOPHIA: What are you up to tonight?

THEO: I don't know

SOPHIA: I'm just, you know,
pampering myself a little.
A face mask and just sitting around
in my robe.

THEO: Oh nice. Sounds cozy.

THEO: Picture? I bet you look so cute.

Sophia might not be straight
but I do know Theo is from this exchange.
No way would a bisexual / pansexual guy
be this freaking boring.

I'm gripping my phone like,
Sophia likes this??? Ugh he's so boring.

Another:

SOPHIA: Do you know what you want to do like in life?

THEO: Not really. Probably become a computer programmer.

SOPHIA: I want to become an actress.

SOPHIA: It's always sounded so romantic a career to me.

I'm also thinking . . . Sophia doesn't actually talk like this
or even believe half the stuff she's saying.
That should be like against the flirting rules.
Or maybe that is the flirting rule?

When I was with Liam, he just kind of asked me.
There wasn't a whole lot of romance to it.
I feel like I should be taking notes here.

I DON'T KNOW EVEN WHERE TO START WITH THIS

I decide to save Theo for last
because it would be weird
if Sophia and I were trying to get with him
at the same time.

I try to focus on myself and who I like.
Who do I actually like?

I think of Pen.
Beautiful Pen.

Pen is kind of friends with Sophia.
She's on the stage crew for all the shows.

She definitely has big
manic pixie dream girl energy
and I love that about her.

I go on her Instagram profile
to scour for some sort of conversation starter.

WHAT DID PEOPLE DO BEFORE THE INTERNET?

I first met Pen when we had a gym class together.
We were like acquaintances.

We had the same gym class and we were the only upperclassmen
in a locker room full of freshman girls.

You'd think we would be in charge or whatever
but these were the cool, stunning freshman girls,

so we were actually kind of scared of them.
It's not that they were outwardly mean, but they would

give us this knowing
you're clearly unpopular and strange stare.

Pen and I stayed in the back for every class and planned
our skip days together. We never talked about anything deep

but I do remember her mentioning that she likes
to run and that she plays *World of Warcraft* on weekends.

I go through her Instagram and it's full of posts talking about
video games I've never heard of. I Google one of the games

and read synopses in case she talks about them.
I feel like I'm studying for a test or an interview

which feels wrong. I don't know how
this is supposed to work. How do you

tell someone you kind of just want to fuck but also
that you appreciate them as a human and

you don't just see them as an object? I don't want
to fall in love with Pen but I want to hold her

and kiss her. Can I even know I want that?
This whole thing was a bad idea.
I can't ask Sophia.
She'd think I'm overanalyzing things.

I'm kind of embarrassed I've never
even really kissed anyone I was into before.

Like yes, I kissed Liam
but I mean like *seriously* kissed.

ODE TO BEING SEVENTEEN

When I feel like I should be falling in love with someone
RIGHT NOW, I try to remind myself
that there's still a lot of time to fall in love.

All around me, though,
everyone I know
seems to be in love
with someone.

My list of friend group couples
keeps growing as summer gets into full swing.

There's Erin and Jorge.
There's Tyron and Alex.
There's Hank and Olivia.
There's Cody and Maureen.

It feels like everyone has a someone.

Especially in the summer,
people I know from school
are just hanging out
with their girlfriends and boyfriends
and partners.

I don't even know if I want
to be in love with someone else.

The only person I've ever really felt that with
is Sophia. I don't know how I'll feel hearing about her
try to hook up with people—
just this bit about Theo is killing me.

I'll have to write down ways I can respond.
I'll have to practice.

I WONDER IF I'LL EVER GET BETTER AT TELLING PEOPLE HOW I FEEL

It's not something
my family usually does.

Actually, I think this whole car crash thing is the most
vocal any of them have ever been.

Even sharing a room with Chris,
we don't talk much. We say "hello"
and "good morning," or whatever. I don't
even tell him when the mess
on his side of the room bugs me.

I just clean it up myself or I push it
to the side. Why do I do that???

CHRIS AND I

The whole time I'm grounded, I keep thinking that I should
at least try to talk to Chris. He's only three years younger than
me.

When we were little, we talked all the time.
We discussed our favorite dinosaurs and what the best ice cream
was.

I know it's probably my fault he doesn't want to talk anymore—
what with blowing him off for the car ride and generally ignoring
him.

It's the last day of me being grounded so I want to try something.

"Hey Chris?" I say.

He's at his desk in our room
and I'm at mine.

    "What?"

I didn't really think this through.
The urge to talk to him just like burst out.

"Do you like anyone?"

Chris turns around.
He looks concerned
and a little annoyed.

"What?" he asks again.

"I'm sorry I didn't mean to be weird.
You just like don't talk to me anymore
and I wondered if it was because
you have a crush on someone."
Which is . . . only partially a lie.
I don't think he doesn't talk to me
because of that but I do think
he might have a crush and honestly
maybe I can learn something from him.

Chris pushes the door shut slowly
with his foot and pulls his chair close to mine.
"Who told you?" he asks
in a stern and serious voice.

"Whoa, no one. I'm just bored
and thinking out loud.
I've been grounded
like all week."

"Wait you're grounded?"

"The car, remember? Duh?"

"Oh yeah . . . that wasn't your fault though, right?"

"It kinda was.
I feel stupid about it."

"Oh, okay."

"You just didn't realize it because you
NEVER get grounded."

Chris shrugs. "This is true."

My parents think Chris
can do no wrong. It's honestly
the most annoying thing.

"But really what are you talking about?" Chris asks.

"I just have a crush on a person
and I wondered if you were like
dealing with anything like that too."

"You're like fifteen, that's when
I started having big crushes," I say.
This is totally just code for
"when I started having
a little crush on Sophia."

I wonder if this is like
beyond what siblings talk about.

Was this weird?

Too late now.

"Do you promise you won't tell anyone?"

"Who would I tell, Chris?"

"I don't know . . . Mom?"

"Never!"

"Not even Sophia?"

My face flushes thinking about Sophia.
"No not Sophia."

He runs a hand through his hair
and looks at the door as if Mom might pop in
at any moment.

"I like this . . . guy."

THANK GOD!

"Chris you're gay!" I say a little too loudly.

Chris's glare could slice a table in half.
"Quiet!" he hisses.

"I'm sorry I'm sorry!
I just got excited!"

"Excited?"

"Because I'm bi!"

"Oh," Chris said.

"Oh?"

"I don't know if I'm gay.
It's just something that's going on."
Chris put his hands up
in defense.

"Tell me about him."

"Wait you're bi? For how long?"

"Haha, how long?"

"Like how long have you known, I mean?"

"Probably a long time but
I like came out to myself
a few years ago."

"Damn, maybe I am gay."

"Haha, runs in the family?"

"When are you going to tell Mom and Dad?"

I pause.
"I actually don't think I'm gonna do that
for a long time."

"Why not? I feel like they should know."

I narrow my eyes.
"Should? No. Chris, come on.
They aren't like bigots but they aren't
pride-parade walkers either.
Why not wait
until I'm like living on my own
and I don't have to worry about
them freaking out?"

"It seems sneaky."

"Sneaky? Chris you didn't
even tell me you like a guy."

"I guess I've just been
feeling guilty about it."

I take his hands in mine and say,
"WE don't have to feel guilty
about anything."

ODE TO ESCAPING

Lars, I miss
being able to tell Mom and Dad
"I need to get something at the store,"
even when
I didn't actually need anything.

Sometimes we'd just drive
to the pharmacy
to look at makeup. Sometimes
we would actually drive
to the supermarket to walk aimlessly
down aisles of cereal or pasta.

I wish I would have invited people
to come with me—even if it wasn't a date.
I guess it just felt
like the only place
I had my own personal world,
I never wanted to bring someone in and change that space.

I keep thinking of all the other trips
we could have taken.

Places I could have gone. People I could have
made plans with.

Lars, how can I
train myself to stop regretting
and start looking again
for places and spaces
to feel that same way,
even though I don't have you?

MEDIUM-SIZED EVERYTHING

"Can we drop this for now?"
Chris asks.

"All right.
All right but just know
you can talk to me about it
any time, okay?"

"Okay," he says.

There's a long, awkward silence.

> He says,
> "All right. I'm going for a walk."

I feel bad. Maybe I reacted too strong.
I imagine him on
our boring street ambling along the sidewalks
of suburbia. The roads swirl around

medium-sized houses
and medium-sized lawns.

There's a yard behind the apartment we live in
but its grass is dried and yellow and the yard is
full of junk so we can't go out there much anyway.

I miss the old apartment. I miss the clean tiles of the bathroom
and the nice, soft gray carpet in the living room.

The carpet here is scraggly and coarse—
brown and speckled.

I wish there was a park with a stream nearby.
A park doesn't really feel like a park without

some sort of lake or creek or river.
I wish Chris didn't have to worry about

coming out. I wish I didn't either.

I wish I would have brought it up
in a less annoying-big-sister
kind of way.

I know Sophia said
that sometimes she feels annoyed
when people are "too into"
her being trans.

I wonder if I'm doing the same thing
to Chris. He didn't even say he was gay.

What if he's bi too and I like
bi-erased my own brother???

All I want to do is sit and face-palm.

FREEDOM

Mom makes shepherd's pie for dinner, which
has been a favorite ever since Chris and I started eating it
for school lunch.

Mom thinks it's gross:
the layer of mashed potato and the layer of once-frozen veggies
and the layer of ground beef and the bread-crumb crust on top.

She makes it for us anyway.

We've only been eating dinner together for a few weeks
because Mom read this study that said families who
eat dinner together have lower rates of teen drug addiction.

This is a perfect example of how Mom overreacts to everything
she reads.

I'm not a scientist but I know that sitting
at our cramped breakfast table is not going to be the difference
between me developing a mental illness or not
(that ship has sailed anyway).

I know it sounds bad but I preferred not having to have
sustained interactions with Mom and Dad.

I don't think they're bad people, I just always feel like
when I talk to them, I'm going to slip up
and say something that'll make them disappointed in me.

Tonight, I focus in and out of conversations.
I'm waiting to double check that I'm un-grounded and

I'm scared to ask because sometimes my parents are the type
where asking could get you grounded longer which I think is
dumb.

Dad hates vegetables so he scrapes that layer off the shepherd's
pie.
Mom only likes vegetables, so she eats the veggies off Dad's plate.

There's a long silence that's killing me
and then Mom says, "I think this shepherd's pie is growing on
me."

Dad teases, "You mean the veggies inside it?"
Mom shrugs and eats a forkful, saying, "Yeah."

I look to Chris, hoping to share a look of commiseration
but he keeps looking down at his plate.

Finally, I manage, "So . . . am I un-grounded yet?"

Mom furrows her brow,
"What do you think?" she asks Dad.

Dad shrugs. "You really did total a car.
My dad would have grounded me my whole life."

"I didn't mean to do it though—
am I going to lose my whole summer
over one mistake?"
Oh no—I think that was too far.

"I'm really sorry,"
I add, hoping that smooths things over.

They both say, "I know," at the same time.

"It's okay if not . . .
I was just checking,"
I say because I know how this goes—
I have to pretend to be super obedient.

It kinda sucks.
I wish I could just say how I feel with my parents
instead of this routine where I act how they want.

"I think that's enough, yes,"
Mom says. "Do you have a plan or something?"

I flush because I was thinking
about Sophia's and my
sexscapade goals.
"Nope, not yet."

Mom scowls. "Claire, is there another boy?"

I panic. I can't tell if there being a boy would be good or bad.
Judging by the previous situation, I would say it would be
terrible.
"No, just a friend."

"Is the friend a boy?"

"I'm not sure,"
I say stupidly.

Dad looks confused. "What?"

"I mean—it's not a specific friend, I just want to hang out
with more people."

They don't seem convinced, but Mom adds,

"Well . . . whatever plans you make,
keep us in the loop."

Which means I'm free!

FLIRTING: TAKE 1

ME: Hey there! I know we haven't talked since we had gym class
together but I've been thinking about you

delete

ME: Hey there! I know we haven't talked since we had gym class together but I really liked hanging out and it would be fun to do it again!

delete
ME: Hey there! Do you remember me from gym class last year? Haha that was a terrible class but we survived together right?

delete
ME: Hey there! Do you remember me from gym class last year?
. . .

PEN: Uhhhh Claire of course I say hi to you all the time what are you talking about
PEN: *gif of a confused dog*

FLIRTING: TAKE 2

ME: Haha I don't know I wasn't sure how to start talking.

PEN: Oh, Claire my wonderful awkward dear.

ME: I wanted to ask if you felt like hanging out sometime.

PEN: Of course! Yeah totally. I'm working at the diner this summer but other than that I'll be bored out of my mind.

ME: Oh cool! Yay!

PEN: What do you have in mind?

ODE TO IMAGINING A *DREAM* FIRST DATE

So much about dates and dating
seems to be about
whether or not your fantasies match up with the other person's.

That's why everyone's always asking,
"What's your dream date?"

I guess I just want
to keep those fantasies for myself.

I feel like if I tell someone—even someone I like—
about them, the fantasies will lose
some of their magic.

I've always thought about going on a hike
along the Perkiomen Trail—stopping at some random
diner or corner restaurant and having dinner there,
still sweaty from walking the gravelly path.

It's not just that sweat turns me on . . .
I also just like that idea
of being exhausted with someone
after an afternoon moving through the trees together.

If I'm being honest right now, the last part
of the fantasy
involves returning to a car by the trail
and having sex in the back seat.

Why do I think car sex is hot? It's weird, right?
Like I guess maybe it has something to do with
the privacy. I know it sounds strange but a car
has always felt more private to me
than a bedroom or a house.

Yes, maybe that's it.
And then there's the added scenery—
the wind blowing through the trees
and the summer-night sounds
of crickets and cicadas blooming
just outside the car windows.

It's like being out in nature
and being safe and secure
at the same time.

I MISS YOU, LARS

Sometimes I wake up and I forget that
you're not here anymore.

I go out in the driveway with my keys
(which I haven't gotten rid of yet).

I stand there
and only see Mom and Dad's car.

I come inside
and I make coffee

and I sit at the table alone.
There're so many more important things

than a car, I know.
My family is alive. I'm fine.

I had a great year with you.
Why does this all make me feel so hopeless?

I guess it's a lot of things.
I like to be perfect

for my parents.
I like to be perfect for everyone.

When I mess up, I find excuses.
Like when I almost failed

environmental science class,
I told my parents that

everyone was almost failing
(which was kinda true),

so I could feel better.
The evidence here is clear.

I broke my own car, I destroyed you.
It was my fault.

There's now a police report
that says it was my fault.

Should I even drive again?
What was I thinking, where did I go wrong?

Where can I find
a space to be myself?

I get up early so that I'm the only one
in the morning kitchen.

I wish we lived in a house like Sophia.
All those windows and doors

and an attic and a basement.
I wish we had more money. It's not like

we don't try so it seems unfair somehow
that other people can have so much space.

Space to fill with boxes. Space to wander.
Space to let their bodies fill rooms.

I wonder what Pen's house is like . . .

WHAT I HAD IN MIND

I don't know what a first date should be
or if it's even a date with Pen.

Girls who like girls are like never direct with each other—
our connections are either
a lightning bolt
    or a slow
        gradual
            falling
                falling
                    falling
                        for each other.

Or, at least,
that's what people say online.

The slow gradual thing is how I've felt about Sophia.
We're not talking about Sophia though; we're talking about Pen.

I'm a mess, aren't I, Lars?

Pen Pen Pen Pen Pen.
We're talking about Pen.

I'm attracted to Pen
but I'm not sure if we'll click
like as people, so
I don't want the date to be too long (in case it's bad).
I also don't want it to be too short (in case it's good).

Before I can even form a thought, Pen messages me.

PEN: I could throw out some ideas too . . .

ME: Yes, please save me from my indecision!

PEN: So, we could like walk along the creek and get food at that shopping place near Wegmans

ME: I would love to!

PEN: Can I ask you something?

ME: Yes!

PEN: Where is this all like coming from?

ME: What coming from?

PEN: You messaging me???

PEN: I mean we've talked but like never hung out

PEN: lol it's not that deep a question

PEN: Just wondering

I CALL SOPHIA EVEN THOUGH IT'S LATE AT NIGHT BECAUSE I'M FREAKING OUT AND I SHOULD HAVE PROBABLY JUST TEXTED HER

"What should I say to her?" I ask.

"Wait what?" Sophia asks. "Context please."

"Pen is asking WHY I want to hang out."

"What? Just say you're into her."

"That's just so scary.
Who does that???"

"If you don't say it outright,
you're both just going to be confused."

"Huh . . . you give good advice for a straight person."

"I'm sure there's stuff I don't know
but I feel like being up-front is the same."

Now I'm just stalling on
messaging Pen back.

"I feel like most straight people aren't up-front either."

"Yeah and it's super annoying . . ."

"Was that it?" she asks.

"Um . . . yeah I'm sorry I freaked out.
I guess I didn't think
she'd be interested."

"Of course she is Claire, you're a cool person . . .
Promise you won't fall in love with her
and leave me."

"Never,"
I say and the thought of what Sophia means
by "leave me" lingers in my mind all night.

I wish I could not like her so much
or that she would say she likes me too
or that something would change.

Maybe Pen will distract me
until I don't even think about Sophia like that anymore.

I know that sounds messed up.
I do actually like Pen—
I just think about Sophia more.

This is so cliché to like your straight best friend!

I guess that's not fair.

I'll change that—to liking your friend
who may or may not be into girls.

I have to just wipe it away somehow.

How long do these things last?

ME: Okay so I guess this is kind of like asking for a date?

PEN: Oh wow sure!

ME: I'm sorry is that weird?

PEN: No, I'm just not out.

ME: Oh, it can be like secret if that's what you're comfortable with!

PEN: Ha! Secretive. You're so funny and really . . .
how did you know??
I've never told anyone.

ME: I wasn't sure I just thought it was worth a shot.

PEN: I thought I was good at hiding it, darn.

ME: I don't think anyone knows honestly; I didn't even know for sure.

PEN: BTW the answer is yes, I'll go.

ME: Sweet!

PEN: Do you drive?

ME: Yes, but I don't have a car.

PEN: That sucks . . . So, I'll pick you up! ☺

SUMMER SUCKS

I know everyone loves summer but I actually
love the school routine a little more than summer.
I always make a summer routine
to make it suck less.

It feels extra hard this year
without you, Lars, and without any space of my own.
How did I ever survive without you before?

I like having something to do.
That's not true . . . I don't just LIKE it . . .
I NEED something to do.

Before I destroyed you, Lars,
I would drive to the trail and run there.
The sound of gravel crunching beneath
my sneakers. The hush of the wind through tree branches.

Now I run on the sidewalk and it sucks.
The sound of a lawn mower. Dogs barking.
It's not that bad, I guess.

Do you remember how in the afternoons,
we used to drive to Valley Forge Park
to write in my journal? Now I just stay in my room
and glare at Chris when he comes inside.

SUMMER JOB I

I'm going to apply to work at everywhere I can find that's hiring
(which isn't many places because most people
line up their summer jobs in May
and I'm starting in June).

Oh, Lars, I know I should have planned ahead
but I was really only focused
on all the fun I'd have this summer

I guess having a job didn't seem as important
until now—seeing as I'm going to have to help
with whatever fines there are from the crash
and on top of that, I'd like to do something besides
walk on the trail and everything costs money.

Usually, I collect odd jobs around town
from Dad's friends—mostly older people
who want some weeding done in the summer
or driveways shoveled in the winter.

At our old apartment,
I used to mow the lawn and trim the hedges
for twenty dollars a week. It wasn't a lot
but it was something.

SUMMER JOB II

I walk up to the host at Rodeo Grille
and I say, "I saw you guys are hiring
for thirteen dollars an hour, I'm interested.
I printed out my resume."

The host laughs and I wonder
if I said something wrong.
I am a little tired from walking.

With you, Lars, this would have been
a five-minute drive but it was almost
a thirty-minute walk.

"I'm sorry, am I confused?" I ask,
certainly sounding confused.

"That's for full time. You're what, seventeen?"
he asks.

"Yeah," I say. "I am but I'm happy to work."

"We start part-timers at nine dollars an hour,"
he says.

"That's not so bad," I say, trying to not sound
too disappointed.

He shrugs. "Okay, fill out an application."
He hands me a paper and I fill it out right there
at one of the booths.

All over the walls are dusty Wild West–themed posters
and knickknacks. The whole place smells kind of like
barbecue sauce. I convince myself it's not that bad
but then I see a burly old guy spit on the floor
and I'm like . . . okay so this is a last resort.

I try to smile when I hand the application in.
I say, "Thank you so much!"

After, I walk twenty minutes to Whole Life Grocery,
which I'm hoping will be better.
It's an organic grocery store
and sometimes I've gotten smoothies there
with my friends.

I go to the customer service desk
and say, "I saw your hiring sign!
I brought my resume—I'm interested."

The lady at the counter sighs.
"Sadly, we just hired the last person we need this summer."

I sigh too and thank her for her time.

The last place I saw with a hiring sign is
the nursing home and by the time I get there,
I'm practically dripping with sweat.

I walk up closer to their hiring sign
and it reads, "Applications online only"
and I feel a little bit of relief.
I need a shower and to just lay on the floor.

SUMMER JOB III

I hope one of the places I applied to calls me back.
I tried restaurants and the golf course
and even the nursing home up the street.

Besides the money, I just want
to get out somewhere and I'm
trying not to be too clingy with Sophia.
I feel like now that she knows I'm bi,
she'd notice the feelings I have for her
and I don't want to bombard Pen
with wanting to hang out all the time
this early on in getting to know her.

PEN PICKS ME UP IN HER SMART CAR

The first thing I think is,
"Who in the world
has a Smart car at seventeen?"

I feel like a weird moment of jealousy
but I shake it off. I don't need a Smart car.
Pen waves from the front seat. Her car

is tiny and bluish gray.
I think if I were going to name him,
I'd call him "Stewart" or "Percy."

Smart cars are cute but also super tiny.
Not a whole lot of room to
you know . . .
do anything sexy in . . .

The car smells new and Pen hugs me
across the seat divider. AC blasting,
both of us are cold to the touch.

I keep oscillating between feeling super anxious
and just enjoying Pen's company.

"Music?" she asks
and hands me her phone,
plugged into the car's speakers.

I panic. This could make or break things,
what if she thinks the music I like isn't cool?

Really, I'd love to play some older Panic! At the Disco
but I feel like I should play a band with a girl lead singer
because idk that just seems more appropriate
for a girl date . . . I'm definitely overthinking this.

"I don't know what to play," I finally admit.
"I usually let Sophia pick the music.
We're like best friends." I laugh nervously.
I didn't mean
to bring up Sophia.

Pen laughs. "Suit yourself—
wahaha I'm in control now."

I watch as she plucks the phone from my hands.
Each of her nails is perfectly painted
the exact color of her shoulder-length teal hair.

Her makeup is so precisely perfect,
it almost looks like it's not real.
Sharp-winged liner and smooth dark eyebrows
with two little slits cut in them.

Where does anyone learn how to look so good???
She doesn't usually wear this much makeup for school
which makes sense—she'd have to get up
at like five to be able to do so much detail.

She taps the play button and electric girls
and loud screaming vocals burst from the speakers.

She shouts over the music to say,
"This band is called GRLwood!
I love them!"

Is Pen too cool for me? She might be.

WE GO TO THE TRAIL LIKE WE'D PLANNED

I take her to all my favorite spots.
We crouch under the bridge
and watch the creek flow past.

I love that Pen can be so into makeup
and hair but then also isn't afraid
to get dirty and play in the woods.

She tells me, "I'm glad you asked me out.
I was starting to think
no one would ever read me as queer
and I'd have to just write
'I'm a lesbian' on my forehead."

I joke, "Straight guys would probably
still ask you out even if you did that."

She groans. "It's true!"

I hold her hand and
this feels like more than
just a date
or a hookup or whatever.

I feel guilty.
I even thought about it
like that—
like a hookup or a fling.

Does anyone really hook up in high school?
Or is that just like a thing in movies?
I don't know but sitting with Pen,
I know that's not what this is—
there's so much chemistry between us.

She makes me feel playful,
the way she's always sweetly teasing
me and herself.

She kisses my hand and my whole body
feels bright and warm.
I feel this flood of emotions—a rush of need.

I want to be with her forever and I know
it's too early for me to mean that
but I tell myself I can be
rational later—

right now I'm just enjoying
being swept away

by this awesome girl.

PEN ASKS

"Who was your first girl crush?
Mine was probably Hayley Williams . . .
but if I go back even further,

I really, really liked Princess Bubblegum,"
Pen says.

"Isn't she like a cartoon character?"
I laugh.

"Yeah I know it wasn't like gross!
Just like if I were also living in *Adventure Time*
I'd have a crush on her. She was a badass scientist.
Come on, you must have had some crushes."

I think really hard
back to the cartoons Chris and I used to watch.
Chris had a hard-core retro cartoon phase he roped me into.
"Oh, definitely the Hex Girls
from *Scooby-Doo!*
If we're sticking with *Adventure Time* though,
I think I had a crush on Marceline."

"Wow I see you have a type," Pen jokes.
"Those are literally some of my outfit references."

"It's amazing how many like
clearly queer girls there were like
in plain sight," I say.

I toss a rock into the creek
    and Pen tosses one too.

BRUSHING SHOULDERS

Gray gravel crunching
under our shoes. Pen stares
up at the trees. Birds laugh and hop
from branch to branch. Rustling. Leaf against leaf.
Hush of car tires on the road nearby.
We walk side by side,
slowly and slowly getting closer together.
Our fingers brush. Our shoulders brush.

I smell her flowery lilac perfume.
She lets her fingers brush
my waist and my thigh. Small touches.
No one else around.
I feel safe out here with her.

YES, YOU CAN HAVE SEX IN A SMART CAR

No room to move at all.
Elbow and elbow and knees.
This all happens
so fast. How come I'm still asking myself,
"Do I really
like girls?" while I pull
Pen's face closer to mine.
I don't really know Pen.
She asks me if I've ever kissed
a girl and I say, "No,
no I haven't kissed
a girl," and she's asking me
if I want to kiss her,
and of course
I want to kiss her,
and she's telling me
she thought she'd have to
wait till college to find another
queer girl and how
I'm gorgeous and
I'm telling her she's
the only girl I'll ever love
and yes, it's too fast to say that
but sometimes you need
to say what feels true
in a moment. We're crawling
into the backseat
of her tiny car

and she's taking off my
white tank top and
pulling her flower print dress
over her head. Her skin
is soft and her mouth
is soft and we are soft together.

INTERRUPTED

I'm focused on her, but in the background I hear the sound
of tires on gravel. "Someone else is in the parking lot!" I blurt

into her face because we're so close.
"Shit!" she says and hands me my shirt from where it got shoved

between the seats. We're laughing nervously and checking to see
if the car noticed us. We joke that no one would suspect

two teenage girls of fucking in a parking lot. We watch
as a man gets out of his car with his fishing rods

and a cooler. Walks to the trail and disappears.
By the time he's out of sight, we're too nervous

to do anything else. She kisses me though
and I kiss her back. We wait there awhile

before she drives me home.

AFTER

It feels strange being in front
of other people

      after being kind of naked in front
    of someone else.

I imagine Pen in my room
alone with me.

I imagine her biting my ear
and telling me a story about when she was little.

I want to know everything about her.
Why does this feeling have to come

so fast?

ODE TO PEN'S CAR

Tight space.
Close bodies.
Blossoming smell of her hair.
Soft fingers.
Teeth and lips.
The metal walls
holding us.

WHEN I GET HOME,

Mom asks, "How was hanging out with your friend?"

I reply (way too quickly), "It was really fine!"

Mom looks confused. "I've never met her before.
Where did you meet her?"

I try to stay cool.
"I took a class with her
and she texted to tell me
she was sorry to hear I was in an accident."

Mom seemed to relax. "That's nice of her. It's good you got
out. You have all summer."

I never know exactly
what answers Mom is looking for anymore.

She pauses a moment before adding,
"You do know you have to pay that fine still.

It's great to see friends but you need to be working.
Pay the fine and start getting ready for college."

"I am working on it.
I will pay you guys back soon."

Mom looks stern.
"Claire, we are not paying that.
You need to pay that fine—
we don't have the money.
Do you think we just have hundreds of dollars
to spare?"

I feel like an idiot.
Of course they couldn't just pay it.
I should have known better.
I just really thought Mom or Dad
had taken care of it for me
to help buy me some time.

Why the hell would Mom tell me like this too?

Couldn't she just say,
"I love you but we can't help pay for this right now"?
Is that so much to ask for?

I already feel terrible.

Mom adds,
"You should try to find a job soon
before they're all taken up."

I want to shout,
"I know that! I'm trying!"
But getting upset never helps.

I know we don't have the money for them to help.
And I know it was my fault.

I hate that something like this was my fault.
But still, couldn't Mom have said it another way?

I feel really terrible that I even spent time
out with Pen instead of trying to find a job
or working or doing anything productive.

Then college? God, Mom is already talking about college?!?

I want to snap back, "What if I don't want to go?"
Or, "Do I get to just be a teenager
or do I have to jump to the next thing already?"

I know it's fucked up but sometimes
I'm like mad that we don't have more money.
Like, why does this have to be
something I'm worried about???

I know it's not their fault but it isn't fair.

Instead, I say, "You're right.
I'll call the places I applied to
again tomorrow."

I want to say something
that might make her proud of me
so I add,
"One place
is the nursing home
up the street."

> Mom nods. "Now that sounds like a very nice job . . ."
> She's silent a few seconds and then drifts back
> to the kitchen table where all our bills
> > are perched in piles and piles
> > > and piles
> > > > and piles.

THINKING OF SOPHIA

I pace around my house for a while trying to get what happened with Pen out of my mind but I just keep replaying the scene which is super weird because my parents are home. It's a Saturday night and that's like super gross to think about anything like that near them.

Then—something changes. I can't be sure why but I start thinking about Sophia. It's awful—the feelings just gush through me. I think of her sprawled out in bed during our last sleepover. I think of her bright lovely laugh—her dark curly hair spilling across the blankets. She always smells slightly like cucumber melon. Ugh I could die.

I should text her.

Or maybe I shouldn't.

ME: heyyy how has your job hunt been?

ME: mine is going so crappy ☹

SOPHIA: I just got hired at Dunkin! Literally just now!

ME: Congrats!!!

ME: Do you get free donuts 👀

SOPHIA: haha I'm not sure I didn't lead with that question in the interview

ME: I'm going to have to visit during your shift

SOPHIA: Oh no pls don't haha I'll get distracted

ME: That sounds like fun

SOPHIA: Isn't Dunkin kinda far from your house

ME: ♪ I'd walk a thousand miles just to see you make donut . . . tonight ♪

SOPHIA: Oh Claire what am I going to do with you haha

I LAY THE PHONE ON MY CHEST

And stare up at the ceiling
in my and Chris's bedroom.

When I was with Pen,
I thought I was starting to get over Sophia

but now it just feels like
what I feel for Sophia
is back worse than ever.

My mind is a photo album
of my favorite moments with her.

Sophia always wears these bright dresses
in the summer and I picture her and me
getting ice cream like we used to all the time last summer.

The wind blows—ruffling the dress—
and she laughs, dropping her ice cream cone,
so we share my strawberry sundae.

WHEN I'M FEELING MAD AT MOM AND DAD

I imagine all the things I'd do differently.
I picture myself as a mom, picking a daughter up
from a car crash. I imagine holding her
and telling her we're just so glad
she's all right. She's crying and I tell her
she doesn't need to worry.
We will take care of everything.

I sit on the front steps of our apartment building
and watch cars go by. I don't want
to be inside. I know it's like technically "fair"
for me to pay for the crash
but it's not fair. I know there are plenty of kids
whose parents would help them pay.

I know there are plenty of parents
who could just buy their kid a new car.

More than the money
or the car, I want my parents to notice me.
Ever since the crash,
I've felt nervous like more than usual
but I don't feel like I can talk about that
because all they're worried about
is the money and grounding me
for like the first third of my summer.

Do they know how that makes me feel?
Why don't I just tell them?

ODE TO GAS STATIONS

I never thought I would miss stopping to fill you up, Lars.
Ew, like how American is it
to miss a gas station?

On our walk, Pen said that most countries
don't need cars like we do in America—
most countries have like trains and buses
that go everywhere and aren't ridiculously confusing.
Pen has been to Germany and Japan and the UK
and Canada and I've literally never even been outside of the
United States.

I miss the little gas station stores.
I would buy myself those peanut butter cracker sandwiches
and eat them alone with you, Lars. I used to think
this was kind of sad but now I think
it was a way of giving myself time alone.

You, Lars, were my protective sphere
where no one else could reach me.
I would watch people enter and exit

the gas station store—noting what snacks
or tools or other things they carried out with them.

I would also make phone calls in gas station parking lots,
which is why I started thinking about them
because I want to call Sophia but I keep feeling weird
calling her in my house and outside,
I feel like anyone could be listening.
Am I paranoid? Maybe. I guess I'm just worried
somehow someone else will recognize in my voice
how much I like Sophia. Yes. That's actually impossible.
I didn't know I was this scared
of being out. What is my problem?
There are queer people on TV now. I guess
it just feels like queerness is something that happens
other places and not here in my town.

I want to call Sophia
mostly for nosy reasons.

I keep wondering if she's met up with Theo yet.

I wonder if she likes him like I like Pen.
I wonder if I like Pen the way I like Sophia.

Can you like two people
in the same way?

FINDING A SUMMER JOB

It's been almost a week since I started applying places
and since my day of applications,
I applied online at the grocery store
and even to Wawa.

There's not a whole lot of options around here
especially within walking distance.

I'm starting to wonder

what's going to happen
if nowhere calls me?

What's going to happen
if I can't make the money
to pay the fine?

I wish this was something
I could just ask Mom and Dad
but I'm scared it's going to scare them

so I just decide to keep applying.

I even try to call the Dunkin' Donuts
that Sophia is working at
but they say they don't need anyone.

Plus, walking forty-five minutes to work
doesn't sound pleasant.

ME: heyy Soph

ME: Are you busy?

ME: I just kind of need to vent

VENTING

When me and Sophia get into "venting" mode,
we always ask each other if the time is good before we get into it.

It's something I always love that we do—
being able to like have boundaries

and still support each other. But, right now,
I kind of hate that we ask permission

because all I want to do
is let all this job-finding stress out

and Sophia isn't responding. She always replies quick.
I'm trying so hard

not to panic but my mind goes straight to thinking,
"What if she's with Theo?"

PACING

I walk back and forth in my tiny bedroom
       while Chris sits at his desk listening to music.
I'm trying to do anything to distract myself
       and it's too freaking hot to go outside
and I know I look crazy but I don't really
       care anymore—I put my headphones in and listen
to the song Pen played in the car—
       I love the loud guitars and screaming lyrics.
When the phone rings, it somehow startles me
       and I nearly throw the thing across the room
trying to pick up. I think it's going to be Sophia calling
       because sometimes she does that for vent sessions.
I scramble to answer the phone
       and it's the nursing home!!!

THEY WANT TO SEE ME FOR AN INTERVIEW TODAY!

A supervisor
from the nursing home
is on the phone
and I try to put on
my professional voice
to accept the interview.

"Thank you so much
for considering me.
I'll be right there."

The woman says,
"You can take your time."

"Not a problem—
my afternoon is free.
Looking forward to meeting you."

We say a cordial goodbye
and I shout,
"YES!"

I get dressed
and rush out.

Chris is like,
"What are you doing???"

I'm like,
"Can't talk—
I'm about to make MONEY!!"

"If Mom asks, where
did you go?"

"Job interview!"

EVERYONE WHO WORKS AT CARING COTTAGE WEARS THE SAME UNIFORM

Green polo shirt.
Khaki pants.

A woman with bleached blonde hair
greets me when I get there
and gives me a short interview
with her and another supervisor.

I'm trying to act cool and calm
and not desperate.

The last question she asks is,
"Why do you want this job?"

I freeze up.
I don't know???
I need money
and this place is a block away.

I stumble at first and I say,
"I appreciate old people and want to help them."

Which makes me feel kind of shitty because,
I mean I do care about old people, sure,

but it's not something I've thought about before.
The women smile and share a look.

They leave me in a meeting room
while they go to write down some notes.

Alone, I'm sure—like 100 percent sure they're going to tell me
to go home
and then send me some vague email rejection.

I look at the pictures of flowers on the room's walls
and try to strategize
about where else I could try to apply
when they tell me "no."

HER NAME IS TAMMY

and she comes back in and says, "Great, you got it."
She hands me a packet of paperwork.
"You start tomorrow.
Does that work for you?"

I'm a little dazed
and it takes me some processing
before I say "Thank you . . .
yes . . . it does . . ."

Does it? Yes. I don't have anything planned tomorrow.

Relief. I feel relief pouring over me.
I have a job?

I have a job!

I STEP OUT INTO THE HOT AFTERNOON

I want to celebrate
but I'm not sure who to call or text.

I want to call Sophia
because she's always there
to say she's proud of me

but she still hasn't texted back
from when I asked to vent earlier.

That's so not like her
and I'm trying not to spiral about it.

I stand in the front lawn of the nursing home
and walk to find a tree to sit beneath.

I could call Mom? But she would just say
something like, "Well good."

I just want
someone to celebrate with.

Maybe I should call Pen?

Would that be weird
since we've only been
on like one date?

I want to call but I think texting
would come off less weird.

ME: Omg! Guess what? I just got a job!

PEN: WHAT! That's great, where?

ME: The nursing home

ME: I know I know it sounds boring but I really think it could be cool

PEN: That doesn't sound boring at all

PEN: I bet people will tell you all kinds of good stories there

ME: I know! That's what I was thinking too!

PEN: That's so cool

PEN: Super happy for you

BUZZING

And just like that
I'm buzzing again—
my whole body
electric
thinking about Pen
and the day we spent together.

Her cool and her laid-back kindness.
The way she made me feel
like I could relax into myself.

It's amazing how
just a few texts
can turn me into
a whole beehive.

HOME

Mom is sorting out salon appointments
on her planner.

I don't want to bother her
but I do want to tell her I got the job.

"Hey Mom?"
I ask, sheepishly.

> Sternly, she looks up
> from her notes.
> "I'm very busy, Claire."

"I got the job,"
I say.

> I can see Mom relax a little.
> "Good."

I wish she would say
something else—

maybe even just
"Good job" or
"I'm proud of you."

Instead of
just "Good."

She goes right
back to work

like I thought she would.

SEVEN A.M.

I start at seven a.m. in the morning,
looking lost as I watch other staff moving this way and that.

The place smells like soup
and laundry—like a home but slightly off.

The whole home is decorated as if it were a giant house.
There's a grandfather clock in the "living room"

and the TV is always on some daytime talk show.

Why does it make me feel really sad? It's quiet
and some people are sleeping in their wheelchairs.

It's not seeing older people that makes me sad,
it's realizing I didn't really know much about
my grandparents besides Jean.
My grandmom lived in a place like this.

I only saw her when Mom would
pick her up and take her to our house for holidays.

I could have probably visited.
She didn't really like me anyway but I could have tried.
Or, maybe, that's just like what I've been telling myself.

They give me my hours for the next few weeks.
I'll work in the recreation room
and the dining hall.

I feel dumb for feeling anxious
about having less time to hang out with Pen
or Sophia but I do,

and for a few minutes after
the orientation I consider calling and telling them
I can't work anymore. I don't know why
I feel like this.

I just don't want to miss out
on time with people. All of a sudden, it feels like

summer is too short and there's not enough time.
I calm down after a little. I remind myself

about the fines. I hear Mom saying,
        "Claire, we are not paying that.
        You need to pay that fine—
        we don't have the money."

My first real day is this weekend.

BAD IDEA

I think this whole hooking-up-with-people thing
was a bad idea.

I was supposed to hang out with Sophia today (Friday)
because it's the only day
she and I are both off work.

She apologized for not responding
for like a whole day
but she didn't say why she didn't respond.

I feel bad that that annoys me.
It's not that I feel like she should always text me right away—
she just always has,
so the change feels really sudden.

We were going to meet up at her house
like we usually do. I was so excited
to just relax together. I've been missing her
so so so so so much.

I even got Dad to agree to drive me
and like ten minutes before we had to go,
she texted me.

SOPHIA: Heyyyy

ME: Leavin soon!

ME: Can't wait!

SOPHIA: Sooooooo

SOPHIA: Yeah I was kinda wondering if you'd be mad if we like
rescheduled.

ME: Oh yeah of course not, what's up?

SOPHIA: Well Theo said that his parents aren't home so he could
like come pick me up

SOPHIA: His parents are like ALWAYS home

SOPHIA: It's a once in a lifetime opportunity

I still don't even know what I actually
want to say to that.

I don't want
to be rude and tell her,
"I was really looking forward to hanging out;
that's shitty of you to cancel,"
even though that's how I felt.

Finally, I manage to type out something.

ME: Oh totally I get it have fun ☺

I am so mad at myself for lying.

But also mad because
if Sophia doesn't know I like her,
then like how can she even know
she's torturing me,
so it's like actually my fault
I'm being tortured.

Ugh I hate this
and my dad is frustrated too
because he's been waiting around to drive me.

I guess I just wonder if this whole thing
is just going to end up
pushing us apart which is dumb because
it was just a random idea—I didn't know she'd take it so
seriously.

I mean I didn't even know
I'd take it so seriously.

DRIVING WITH DAD

I ask Dad if he wants to go for a ride with me
even though I don't need to go anywhere.

He looks confused but he agrees.
As he grips the steering wheel, I look at his knuckles

and the calluses on his fingers.
They bloom on the sides where they

brush against each other. Dad has always had
rough hands. He used to do odd construction jobs

before he started truck driving.
Back then, he'd come home with tar smudges

and dirt all over his face. I want to ask him
if he notices the calluses

but instead, I focus on trying to tell him
things he might be proud of me for. I tell him

about the new job and he nods as I do.
The drive reminds me of when I was younger

and Dad and I would drive to Valley Forge
or the Philadelphia outlets together to visit a discount bookstore.

"I'm sorry I haven't talked to you much lately," I say.
I don't exactly mean to say it—it's just all I'm thinking about

as we ride up the street and past Target.
Dad waves his hand

as if to say *it's all right*. I don't even know
if I'm really sorry about that specifically.

I think I'm really just feeling down
and alone in my family.

Maybe I'm sorry for growing up. It's happening
too fast and too slow.

Dad says, "This is nice, we should do this more often."

I say, "I course."

Dad says, "I'm so glad you were okay after the accident.
I've thought about how lucky we are every day."

And I don't know what to say
so, I just say, "Sorry."

I try not to think about the crash. Broken glass
and crushed metal.
I wish he wouldn't have brought it up.

Dad says, "It's okay. I'm not upset.
Just happy you're all right."

"SORRY"

When I say "sorry,"
the word has a million meanings.
It depends on the person too.

"Sorry" can be
"I don't know what to say"
or "I feel guilty"
or "I made a mistake"
or "This is uncomfortable"
or "I wish my life was different"
or "I wish your life was easier."
or "I hear you."

So then why
do I always say "sorry"
when I mean
something else?

A NIGHTMARE

I keep crashing cars over and over.   I run into
Sophia. I run into Dad and Mom. I run into
the houses of friends
    who I haven't talked to since middle school.

I run into   the porch of the nursing home.
Everyone is so disappointed in me.   I am a monster.
    I crash into
Pen's car.   I crash into the scene of me and her
messing around in her crammed front seat.

I wake up gasping.
I stand up in the dark of my room.
I breathe in and out.

I WISH I COULD

I wish I could text Sophia
but it's almost three a.m.

I wish I could text Pen
but we don't know each other
that well yet.

I am completely
alone here.

FIREFLY CATCHING

I think it's the most fun when you don't plan on hanging out—
when it just happens suddenly,

especially in the summer,
when there's no school to get in the way.

Sophia texts me that she wants to go firefly catching
in her yard like we used to do when we were little.

We haven't done it since at least middle school
and a part of me hopes this means

she's done with Theo and only wants me
which I know is silly and a little dramatic

especially because like . . . I also still like Pen.
Mom drives me and gives me a speech

about how she's had a long day
and how she wishes she didn't have to drive me.

I feel so guilty.
Growing up is unfair.

I'm caught in this time where I need more freedom
but I have to always ask my parents for it.

I'm lucky they like Sophia.
I've always wondered
if they would trust her still
if they knew she was trans.
I like to hope they would

but I'm not sure.
I've never really heard them
talk about trans people.

I reply to Mom
just saying, "I'm sorry."

    She says, "It's fine,"

and we drive to Sophia's house
in awkward silence.

I roll the window down a crack
and feel the cool twilight air across my face.

When I get there, Sophia has mason jars
with holes poked in the lids all ready to go.

I almost forget I'm supposed to be mad at her
for ditching a few nights ago—I'm just so ready

to be with her again. Oh, Lars, I am
such a mess for this girl. I don't think this is going to end.

WE SHARE MEMORIES

Sophia says,
"Do you remember
the time we tried to walk to Phoenixville?"
(A whole town over.)

I laugh,
cupping a firefly
in my hands
and swearing
the bug feels warm
like a lightbulb.

I add, "We realized it was actually really far away.
But we just kept going for it,
didn't we?"

"Mom had to come pick us up
and our legs were so, so sore."
Sophia laughs and shakes her head.
"I barely can be talked into walking to Wawa."

WE FILL OUR MASON JARS

They glow	brilliant	greenish-yellow
and I'm more	fascinated than	I've ever been
by their bodies'	ability to produce light.	I think about
how Sophia's brown eyes	also glow—	luminous

in her porch light.   I want to forget   about the plan for now

and just   appreciate   her.

AM I JEALOUS OF THEO?

Sadly, Sophia isn't over Theo,
he was just busy tonight
and it stings when she says,

　　　　"Yeah he just had plans tonight."

When did I become
her second option?

Sophia's never made me feel like that before.

I feel like he's taken Sophia from me

and it's not that different
from how I felt after the crash—

like losing you, Lars. She was like
my biggest support system

and now it feels like
she doesn't care.

How can things change
so fast?

I HATE BEING JEALOUS LIKE THIS

　　　　She asks me,
　　　　in the bright and sweet way
　　　　she always does, "How are you?
　　　　It's been a lot these last few weeks, huh?"

I want to tell her about my date with Pen
but I don't want her to think I haven't missed her.

Why am I like this? It's like
there's always a buzzing inside me—

it's either Pen or Sophia or both.

I shrug and say,
"You know—it's a lot
but I'm hanging in there."

        "No progress on . . . the plan?"
        she says coyly.

"Not much,"
I lie, deciding to keep
Pen and me a secret
for at least a little longer.

WE DRINK LEMONADE

The weird powdered kind.
Swirl our spoons
in Sophia's pink glass cups.

Ice clinks against the sides.

"So how's stuff been with Theo?
Ready to cross him off the list?"
I joke.

I am just dying to know more.

        "Can I admit something?"
        Sophia asks.

"Haha sure."
I'm terrified.
I grip the glass
so hard it might break.

"I think I like him more than that . . .
Is that bad?"
She giggles.

I try to mask all the feelings
churning inside—
the feeling I'm literally
going to combust.

"Of course not!
That's awesome."

"I didn't think we'd click like that,"
she says.

"Honestly I didn't either
but then again I don't know him."

"He's really sweet.
I've been like wanting someone
since Alex and I broke up."

"I didn't realize that was that serious;
it was only eighth grade,"
I joke again,
this time feeling
the world slipping out
from under me.

"Yeah but I felt lonely after
and it sucked."

"I get that,"
I say even though I'm thinking,
"BUT YOU HAVE ME!"
I know it's not the same.
BUT YOU HAVE ME, SOPHIA.

Lars, how can she not get it?
I'm like practically begging her
to marry me with how I look at her.

"And you won't believe what else?"
she says.

"What?"
I ask, trying to act like
this is just
a normal conversation.

> "I told him I'm trans!
> I haven't done that with someone
> I *like* like before. AND he was
> super nice about it. He said he
> thinks that's kind of cool!"

Ew, that's a weird way to put it.
I mean Sophia is sooooo freaking cool
but saying her being trans is "cool"
is kind of cringe.

I guess it's not really my job to decide
what she does or doesn't like
but still.

"I'm so happy for you, Soph,"
I say and I take her hand
and we swing it back and forth.

> "What about Pen?"
> she asks, raising her eyebrows.

That lightens the mood.
I do like Pen.
I do have Pen and
I'm really enjoying
getting to know her.

I guess I should tell Sophia
so I don't sound super boring
and now that I know
she's in deep with Theo.

"Honestly kind of same.
I like Pen a lot,"
I say.

"So, we're calling the plan off?
Right?"

I laugh.
"I think so, for now."

I don't know
whether to be relieved
or to be devastated by it all.

STRAIGHT BEST FRIEND

It's such a trope to like your straight best friend.
I can't believe I'm letting it get in the way of liking Pen.

Do I do this on purpose? Ruin things?
Just like I crashed you, Lars, my perfect beautiful car?

I mean, yeah you were old and yeah you made a weird noise
when I turned the key but you would have lasted years.

All the places I could have gone with you.
And now look what I've done! With this stupid plan,

I literally encouraged Sophia to meet someone else.
I mean I wasn't SOMEONE in the first place but still.

I wish I could talk to Mom about this.
Do other people talk to their moms about stuff like this?

She talks all the time
about how her clients

tell her their deepest secrets while sitting
in the salon chair. Mom takes pride in being part stylist-

part counselor. So why is it so hard
for me to talk to her?

Maybe she'd even be cool
with me being queer

if I just gave her a chance.

PART 2

Odes to African Violets

NURSING HOME DAY 1

My first day I expected someone to train me but they kinda just
threw me in.
I'm so anxious about messing something up which is dumb
because
the residents seem surprisingly chill.

I help heat canned green beans and make instant mashed
potatoes for lunch.
Carrie, the woman who runs the kitchen, gives me a tray to take
to some residents' rooms who don't come to the cafeteria.

I should ask her why they don't come but I forgot
and now I'm reading the numbers on the rooms to find
someone named Miss Alberts. I peer in the open doorways

as I walk. Each room looks like a mix between a hospital
and a bedroom and a hotel. It's strange. Sometimes the rooms
look sad
but sometimes they have pictures and vases with flowers.

Finally, I find room 807 where I'm delivering this tray.
Miss Alberts has an iPhone in her lap and her headphones in.
I don't know why I thought old people didn't use iPhones

but it catches me off guard. I don't want to scare her so
I try to wave my hands to get her attention. She eventually
notices me.

    "Grub!" she says and laughs.

"Haha yeah."

    "And who are you?"

"I'm Claire."

    "Ah, nice name. I'm Lena."

I nod, not sure what do to.

"Do you have more work to do?"

"Yeah I think so."

She beams. "Do you want to skip it for a second?"

I glance over my shoulder.
There's no one around.
"Yeah I mean sure!"

"I'll tell them I asked for your help."

LENA IS AMAZING

She tells me to have a seat and
I sit next to her on her
squeaky box spring.

Taking out her iPhone,
she shows me a pug puppy video compilation.

We laugh. She tells me she used to have a dog
just like those. She looks a little sad
so I ask her to tell me
about her dog. She goes on and on about
how she used to take her dog everywhere:
to the movies, to the library, to the park.
She says, "Everyone on my block knew
Winston and he'd stop at each house
to say hello."

I want to stay in her room forever.
It's weird but I feel like we're friends???
Like I would enjoy hanging out with her.
Maybe that's not weird?

"You should go back to work right?"
she asks all of a sudden.

"I want to stay a little longer,"
I say.

She smiles.
"All right. Can I tell you another secret?"

"I mean sure!
. . . Are you this awesome
with every person who works here?"

She laughs. "Of course not!
I hate everyone here."

I know she's joking
but it feels kind of serious.

"Oh no . . . I'm sorry.
Is there something specific they do?"

She shrugs. "They just don't pay attention.
Sometimes I feel like I'm someone's job
here and not a real person.
I know I need help and I know my memory
is all over the place but everyone here
is a full person."

"I see . . ."
I feel so bad. I can't imagine
what it's like to feel
invisible in the home you live in.

"I'm trying this," she says.
She holds up her phone.

It's a dating website!
Oh my gosh! She's on a dating website!
"Wow! Are you talking to anyone?"

She sighs. "No . . . not really.
I've never found another dyke on OurTime."

My eyes go wide.
Once she says it, I notice the signals.

Her short butch hair buzzed to the sides.
Her denim vest—

how did I not notice that?
I guess I just
don't think about older people being queer.

Oh my God,
how did I manage
to meet this woman?

TWO QUEER PEOPLE

"How do you know I'm queer?"
I ask.

> Lena laughs. "I'm old enough to have a sense."

"Gaydar? Haha."

> "No no. It's more than that.
> It's like feeling home . . .
> You must be pretty terribly late now.
> I don't want to get you in trouble, dear,
> why don't you come back again?"

"I'll come when my shift is over!"
I say. "If that's okay,
I'm sorry I just assumed you weren't busy.
I know you probably have stuff to do!"

> "No—no! Ha!
> You assumed right!"

WORKING

It feels good to have a job   mostly because I have something to do.

I feel useful to my family.   I *do* think it's sad that

I only feel useful to them   when I'm earning money

       or getting good grades or something.   Maybe
       being useful

is just overrated.   I just want to exist and relax.

Does anyone my age   really relax?

   I don't know anyone who does.

Sophia's even busier than me: She works
       and does school
       and band
       and theater.

I check my phone on my break.

Pen texted me to ask if I'm busy   after work today.
I want to see her

but I told Lena I would say hello.   Do I actually want to talk to
Lena

more than I want to see Pen?

Ugh that's weird.   I just feel like I haven't had

a friend since   Sophia and Theo got together.

   It's just too weird to talk to her because

I still have all these feelings   and all she wants to talk about
       is him him him him.

   Everything about him!

   His hair   and the song he wrote her

and the date they're going on   and blah blah blah

Ugh it's always back to Sophia.

Why don't I just focus on Pen???
       Pen actually wants to hang out!

I'm just going to ask her

to hang out another time.

Time moves fast and slow at work.

I look at my phone for the time   and it's two more hours
          I look and   it's only been three minutes
                    I look and   my shift is over!

LENA'S ROOM

The door is slightly ajar,
so I push it open and walk in slowly.
This time, I scan her room for details.
I notice a picture of a violet flower on the wall.
I notice a stack of books on the nightstand. I find no family
pictures.
I also realize that her room is one of the few
without two people.

She's asleep. It's been a few hours
and the sun is starting to set
but you wouldn't know it from her room
because there's no window.

"Lena?"

She nearly jumps up. A book is open on her lap.

          "You got me!" She laughs.
          "I'm asleep on the job.
          Back so soon?"

"I wanted to say hi before I go."

          "That's nice of you. Come sit down."

Her room smells different than
other people's rooms.

Almost like incense which is
unique for the nursing home.

"I like your room," I say.

> "Oh, thank you.
> It could use more decorations.
> I've been here for two years
> and still haven't managed
> to do much."

"Oh, why not?"

> "If I decorate too much it'll feel too sad.
> I miss my little apartment in Fishtown."

I shift uncomfortably on Lena's bed.
I just wish I could
like make the nursing home feel less
sterile for her.

She deserves to have
a pretty room.

"That does sound nice.
Can I bring you anything
to make it look more like it?
I totally understand
if it's just too hard—
if it just makes you sad."

> "Oh no, it was mostly the people
> that made the apartment anyway."

"I see."

> "Do you have grandparents?" She asks.

I don't know why I flush but I do.
Does she think I like . . .
want her to be my grandma???

"I did have a grandmom
but she passed away,"
I say.

        "Do you miss her?"

I lie . . . "Yes."
I never really knew my grandmother
but it sounds crappy to say
"No, I don't miss her."
It's not that I didn't care about her
we just never really had a chance to connect.

        "You can come here anytime."

"I'm not visiting you because I miss her though.
I'm visiting you because you're nice
and I hope this isn't like weird but like
we could be friends?"

Why did I ask like that???
I'm so awkward
no one asks to be friends
you just start being friends.

        She seems surprised by this and she nods.
        "Oh . . . yes that sounds nice.
        You have to know, dear,
        people don't visit me
        so I get a little guarded.
        I've had many many friends
        come and go."

"I promise I'm not just saying this.
You're really funny. I'll visit when
I'm not on my shifts too,"
I promise.

I want to ask why no one visits her
but it doesn't seem right.

I mean I don't really know her yet
but there's so much
I want to know about her.

> "Just know you don't have to.
> I'm old, I understand,
> and you're young and busy."
> She smiles. "When I was younger—
> your age—I was ALL over the place."

"No, I mean it!"

> She rests her head in her hands.
> "So all right then, do you want me to
> tell you a story? I always love telling stories."

"Omg, of course I do!"

AFRICAN VIOLET

I used to love this girl.
We flirted but never really
got together. I think about
her a lot these days because
she left the city too.

She writes to me sometimes.
Her letters are jumbled
maybe from being out of practice
or from her starting to lose her memory
or maybe just because
she's still falling for me
after all these years.

Sometimes in her letters,
she writes like
we're back in the '80s.
Sometimes it's 2019.

There's no telling where she'll take you.
That's not the story though.

The story is that she gave
me African violets each time
she visited. Little potted flowers.

I always killed them by overwatering them.
Poor poor flowers. She never got upset though;
she would just tease me and buy me another.
It's hilarious. How many flowers
we went through in that time
when we almost dated but never did.

OVERWATERING

After I leave,
my brain is full
of Lena's African violets.

What must it have been like
to have been friends for so long
and not been able to admit

to liking each other?
I wanted to ask her more questions
but all I could say was that

her story was like a poem—
each line still lingering in my head.
I feel scared that one day

I'll think of Sophia like Lena thinks
about her friend. I'm worried that
I'm going to overwater

my and Sophia's friendship
and that eventually we'll just drift apart.

I'll have to think
of a question to ask Lena
to see if she has any advice.

A FEW DAYS PASS AND

I get in the routine
of visiting Lena after work.

She never runs out of stories.

Some of them are sad and some of them
are bright and some of them
are hilarious but they're all
wonderfully queer.

Somehow, they make me feel
less alone—like being a young queer girl
is nothing new. I tell her about
the car crash and she tells me how she also
crashed her first car—how she still misses
that freedom especially now that she can't drive.

Lena grew up nearby in Macungie
and moved to the city when she graduated.

I'm still trying to work myself up to
asking her for advice about Sophia.

PAYCHECK

Today I got my first paycheck
and I can't believe
I've already worked there two weeks.

I haven't seen
Sophia or Pen at all.
But I do text Pen
pretty much every day now.

I've only texted Sophia
a few memes though.

When I think about it too much,
I start to panic
that in a matter of
a few weeks,
I'm like losing
my best friend.

Am I a bad friend
for not trying to get her attention more???

Have I ditched my friends
for an old lady???

I mean Lena is also my friend
but you know what I mean, Lars.

It does suck though that
most of the money for this first paycheck
is going to go to this stupid car bill.

In my head, I've been calling it
your funeral bill, Lars.

At least this money might make my parents happy
because I took care of it all by myself.

Maybe with the rest of the money,
I can pay for another date with Pen!

WHATEVER-TEXTING

"Whatever-Texting" is what I call texting
when no one is really saying anything.

That's what I've been doing
with Pen this last week at least.

I'm trying to break out of it
but I can like never think of anything to say.

It goes something like, "Hey there how are you?"
and the other person is like, "Good how are you?"
and I'm like, "Good," and the conversation
kind of stops there.

I know I should put in like a tiny bit more effort,
especially when Pen is texting me paragraphs
about watching a movie with her parents
and going out to get ice cream with her sister,
but I'm just like, "That sounds nice."
I can't think of what else to say.

Am I avoiding getting deeper with her?
What's wrong with me?

DINNER TABLE

I show off my first paycheck. I was hoping
Mom or Dad or even Chris would be
impressed but

      Mom just says, "Finally,"
         and Dad says, "That's great,"

between bites of canned corn.

Dad jumps into telling a story
about how he started working before
he was thirteen with his dad, painting houses—
how the primer would get stuck under his fingernails.

Chris doesn't say much of anything.
I don't know why we don't seem to ever
celebrate anything in my family.

Everything is serious or a complete joke.
      Mom says, "Now you can
      finally pay that ticket." I can tell

this is a relief. I feel bad that
I might have caused her more stress but
I'm also angry that no one wants to be excited for me.

I tell everyone I feel sick
and I go to our room
without finishing the casserole or
the watery corn Mom made.

Whenever I'm hungry, I cry easier.
I get this rush of anger at them—
everyone not talking at the table.

The tears are hot on my face
and I lie in bed. I wonder to myself
if Lena's family was like this—

if maybe she grew apart from them
and that's why she moved away
right after she graduated
and that's why no one comes to visit her.
That just makes me more upset.

They don't deserve her
if they did abandon her.
Lena is awesome.

I pull the pillow over my head.
I'm being dramatic; I hate this.

That's when Chris comes in.

CHRIS CAN BE A GOOD BROTHER SOMETIMES

He sits down on my bed next to me
and puts his hand on my back.

"Are you feeling all right?" he asks.

"No," I say.

"Do you want to talk about it?"

I'm surprised he asks.
Usually, Chris doesn't like to talk about
anything upsetting.

Or, maybe it's just because
I've never really checked in
with him
until we came out
to each other.

I wonder if
we both just needed
to come out to each other
to connect again.

"I guess."
I sit up and look at him.

I realize he's really growing up.
He's still my younger brother but
he's tall and in that moment,
he looks so much older.
When did he get so old?

"What's going on?"
Chris asks.

"I don't know.
It's stupid really."

"No tell me!" he says.

I tell him
how sad it made me feel
when no one was excited for me about
my paycheck. I tell him that I wish

our family celebrated
every once in a while

and I worry
I won't ever feel as close to Mom and Dad
as I did when we were younger.

Chris says he feels that way a lot too.

He says, "I'm sorry
I didn't say anything either
at dinner."

That's when someone knocks
on the door.

WHEN WE WERE YOUNGER

Mom and Dad were still strict
and over-worried
but we were kids
so it was more normal
for them to come everywhere with us.

They came to every school carnival
and every school parents' night
and every concert
or show the school put on.

When I was younger,
I felt like they really
would do anything for me.

I felt so loved.

I think it's a combination of things
that make me feel so far from them.
Money is tighter
and money is always stressful.

But, also, both me and Chris
want more freedom
and that's something Mom and Dad
are like too scared of us having, I think.

MOM

Mom stands there in the doorway.
She looks concerned
and scans the room and our faces.

> "Are you feeling okay?"
> she asks.

"I'm fine."

> "Are you sick?" she asks.

How can she NOT know???
I'm obviously upset!

I want to make it easier to deal with though
so I say,
"Just a little nauseous."

> "I'm sorry . . .
> Well . . . if you need anything,
> let me know."
> Mom looks down
>   at the floor.

She stands there for a moment or two.
She looks to me and Chris

as if she's searching
for some more evidence.

I swear Mom notices everything
and she can see

Chris and I were talking about something
we didn't want her to hear.

"Be good," she says with a sigh.

Which is her way of telling us
she knows we're
"up to something."

CAN YOU BE IN LOVE WITH TWO
PEOPLE AT ONCE?

Pen and I decide
we're going on another date
this Thursday

and I'm so excited I barely sleep
    the night before.

Besides just worrying
about being cool enough around Pen,

I'm also nervous
I'll start thinking about Sophia again
    when I'm with Pen.

That's messed up right?

EVERY DAY IN THE SUMMER FEELS
LIKE SATURDAY

I don't ever sleep in
but I do lay in bed till ten some days.

The day of our date
is one of those days.

I think about how
if I had you, Lars,
things might be easier.

I'd love to offer
to pick Pen up this time.

I keep looking at my phone
but I avoid texting her;

I like it when
she texts me first.

PEN: Hey there! Can't wait to see you later 😊

ME: Hi! See you soon!

I don't know
what else to say.

I hate texting because
not texting back sometimes feels like

sitting next to each other
and not talking—

but also when I'm like
not next to someone.
All my thoughts just seem random
and not good for texting convos.

PEN: How are you today?

ME: Great!

Damn why did I text that?
How is she supposed to respond to that?

ME: I'm lazy and I haven't gotten up yet.

PEN: Oh wow! I get up at like six or seven.

PEN: Conditioning from school

PEN: Need time to do my makeup and straighten my hair lol

ME: I wish I could do that!

PEN: How do you get up for school then?!?!?

ME: With a lot of alarms haha

ME: *screenshot of a whole wall of alarms*

HOLDING HANDS

I pay for Pen and me to Uber to the Providence shops.

I feel proud of this even though I miss
being able to drive there myself with you, Lars.

At least with this, I feel like
I'm treating her to something
even if I can't drive her myself.

As we walk in and out of stores,
Pen and I hold hands
and she tells me about her family—
        "I came out last year
        to just my family.
        At first my mom cried."

"Oh gosh . . .
that sounds intense."

        "She was asking me
        if she had done something wrong.
        It hurt . . . it did," Pen says.

"What did you say?"
I ask.

        "Nothing . . . I couldn't really
        find the words.
        My dad told me

I just hadn't found
the right guy."

"I can't imagine how much
that must have hurt to hear,"
I say.

We're standing in Five Below,
fiddling with discount nail polish

as some tweens dart
between aisles.

"It's better now!
Later this month my parents offered
to go to Pride with me.
Haha . . . not sure if it's cute
or annoying."

I can't imagine
my parents coming around so quickly.

I feel jealous
kind of like I feel jealous
of Sophia's parents.

How did everyone but me
get so lucky?

But I don't say that . . .
I say, "That's great! Haha
hope they're prepared."

"Don't worry.
We're going to the one in Phoenixville;
it's very PG rated."

"Oh good—haha!
I was picturing your parents
running into some leather daddy."

"Oh God!!!"
Pen laughs.
"They're not prepared for that."

WE END UP AT THE BOOKSTORE

Pen tells me
she wants to find a new book of poetry.
    Pen says, "Poems help me
    work things out in my head.
    I write some
    but they're all crap,
    so I mostly just
    read them."

All I know about poetry,
I know from a few units in English class.

I don't even know
if what I write
is like really poetry
because I just kind of
share my thoughts and emotions.

Pen tells me her favorite poets right now
are Sylvia Plath and June Jordan.

Pen reads poems aloud to me
from the tiny poetry corner
of the bookstore.

In her voice,
the poems come alive.

I close my eyes when she reads,
so the poems can swirl around me.

    Pen asks, "Are you bored?"

And I say,
"No, I just like
to focus on the words."

> Pen grins.
> "I love that!
> I'm going to try that sometime."

"Do you want me to read?"
I ask, a little shy.

> "Yes please!" she says,

and I do.

SITTING IN COMFY BOOKSTORE CHAIRS

I try to read a book of poems
by Sharon Olds.

Pen recommends her to me
because she wrote a lot of ode poems
and I told her I love odes.

Mostly, I can't focus
with Pen sitting next to me
all curled up with a book
of haikus.

I lean over to her
and we kiss again
but this time
it's more romantic than sexy.

We scoot our chairs
closer. How ridiculous
are we?

She's leaning on me—
resting her head
on my shoulder.

ODE TO IMAGINING A DIFFERENT ENDING

We both have to take separate Ubers home
because it's getting late.

I sit in the back seat and the whole ride
I think about how cute it would have been

for me to drive Pen home with you, Lars. I would have
parked and then kissed her one last time

before going home. I would have played
my favorite radio station and maybe they'd play

a song we both like. It could become
"our song" or something cheesy like that.

I know it's dumb to be so upset about losing a car
but sometimes I feel so trapped without Lars.

I can't have my parents drop me off on dates—
especially with a girl! I just know there're

so many teenagers who will never have a car
and adults who can't afford one either.

It's not fair how much you need one
to get around my town. On our date Pen said

we should figure out the buses and I think
I'm going to do that. Maybe my parents

were so upset about the car because
they won't be able to get me another one—

because they only have one car between
the two of them. We got a FREE car and I ruined it.

I should stop blaming myself. I just feel
so guilty. I wish everything didn't like always come back
to this stress over money.
I wish it was easier for us.

BACK AT HOME IN BED

I scroll through my phone and
Sophia texts me.

This surprises me
because I expect it
to just be another meme or something
but it's not.

SOPHIA: Hey

ME: Hi! What's up?

Do I play it cool?
Or, do I let her know
I miss her.

I should be honest.

ME: I haven't seen you in forever

SOPHIA: haha it's only been like a week?

ME: two weeks

Ugh now she knows I'm like counting.

I don't want to sound clingy.

But we're best friends!

We've always been clingy before.

ME: that's forever!

SOPHIA: Maybe this weekend?

ME: Sure!!!

Too many exclamation points.
Ugh, Claire, get it together.

ME: I work Saturday but Sunday I'm free!

ME: How's life been?

SOPHIA: Complicated . . .

ME: Oh?

I don't want to be too nosy
but Sophia's always been
pretty open about things so I ask . . .

ME: What's been going on?

Do I push it more?

Yes. Yes I need to know right now.

ME: Is it about Theo?

SOPHIA: Sort of

SOPHIA: We'll talk more when I see you

SOPHIA: How r u?

ME: Good! I actually like my job

ME: I have so much to tell you about it.

SOPHIA: About working at the nursing home? Lol sounds invigorating

ME: you won't believe it!

ME: It actually is!

TAKING THE BUS

I get coffee with Sophia at Starbucks.
I learned how to use the bus to get there and it took forever with
all the stops
but I felt pretty proud that I figured it out.

Would it be so hard to have more buses?
How do people without cars
even get to work? It's like the system is designed to make life harder.

That's not to say I don't appreciate you, Lars.
Cars are just expensive and I don't think
people should like have to have them to get around.

SOPHIA AND THEO

Sophia spends the whole first half hour talking about her and Theo
and all the while I just sit there, slowly dying.

> "You know how I like . . . never break rules?"
> she asks, looking mischievous.

"Haha yeah,"
I say. I'm also thinking
that it's hard to break rules
because her parents don't have many.

> "So, on Thursday
> I snuck Theo over to stay the night!"

"Did you have to like
help him in the window?!
How did you do it?"
Trying to sound excited for her
when really I just feel panicked.

> "Yes! Ha! How ridiculous, right?
> I just HAD to see him, you know?"

"Mhm," I agree.

> "Then! THEN! I SNUCK OUT!
> Last night I stayed at his place
> and my parents don't even know,"
> she brags.

I'm thinking about
how there is absolutely no way
in hell my parents wouldn't notice that.

> "I figured if they found out
> I'd just tell them I was staying
> with you," she says with a shrug.

"Were you going
to tell me? Give me a heads-up?"
I ask, trying to sound
like I'm teasing
and not actually hurt.

I do feel hurt. I mean
it's one thing
to use me as your alibi
but to not even tell me???

> "Theo's family is so chill.
> They didn't care if me and him were alone,"
> she says.

I'm kind of jealous
she's having such an easy time
finding space with Theo
when I don't feel
like I can ever find that
with Pen.

"Whoa that's awesome,"
I say. Then, more honestly, I add,

"God, I wish my parents
were like that."

I don't know if I totally mean it though.
I don't think I'd like it if
my parents just totally didn't care
what I did. I guess I want

some sort of balance.
Really though, who knows
what I want.

CAN BEST FRIENDS GROW APART THIS FAST???

She tells me about how they haven't had sex in his car yet
but they want to.

I say,
"I can't believe both our partners started off
as some weird game trying to hook up with people
in their cars."

        "I know, right.
        I kind of love it!" Sophia says.

She's looking at her phone now
which didn't used to bother me
when we were hanging out

but now it does—I know
she's texting Theo.

        "Sorry," she says.
        "He gets anxious
        when I don't text back."

I'm thinking,
"Uh hello! So do I!"

She finishes and puts the phone down,
taking a big sip of her Frappuccino,
which Sophia always calls "fancy milkshake."

> "I miss you. I'm glad we're here,"
> Sophia says, opening her phone again
> after it vibrates.

It doesn't feel
genuine.

If she really misses me,
why don't we just
hang out
like we used to?

I can't put my finger on why
but you know how
sometimes people say something
because it's what they feel like
they should say?

It felt like that, Lars.

I worry that after this summer,
Sophia won't be my best friend anymore.

I know that sounds dramatic but I feel like
this past month we've been weird and
I don't feel like I know her anymore.

Was it this whole thing? Is it Theo
who's making her different? Is it Pen
who's making ME different?

Maybe I'm just worrying more than I need to.

People can't be like constantly clicking right?

This is normal, right? Right?

ODE TO LAST SUMMER

Last summer,
things felt so easy with Sophia.

Almost every day,
we would get up and set off

on a mini adventure together.
I just want that back

and I hate how our jobs
and our lives are getting in the way.

It feels like everything is
pulling us apart.

I always thought growing up
would be freeing

but all the responsibility
of trying to save money

and trying to be a good daughter
and trying to plan for the future

feels like a trap—not like any kind
of freedom.

ME: It was really nice to hang out!

ME: Maybe we can next week

SOPHIA: Yeah maybe!

NURSING HOME SHIFT

Things can be

chaotic   and then quiet.

There is no   in-between.

I start to learn everyone's names.

Doris is sweet and knits all day.

> Greg only eats mashed potatoes.

Elaine doesn't like me because I remind her of her daughter.
> She'll call me "Lisa."

> Ike plays chess with himself.

George yells if you don't read the bingo number fast enough.

> Louise paints watercolor sunsets.

Lena doesn't go to the social events
> and when I ask her why, she waves her hand and says,
> "We can talk about that later."

I guess I shouldn't have asked her
while we were sitting
in the dining room
where other people can hear us.

All of this makes me wonder what I didn't know
> about my grandmom.

I wish I would have visited her more.
> I feel guilty about it.

It's like these people's whole world
> is hidden away inside this building.

BUT I—

Today, I bring some old paintings
I did in art class last year
to add some more color to her walls.
> She says, "No, no you don't have to
> give these to me."

"But I want to!"
I say
as I help her hang
the pictures—
one on each wall.

We sit down
at her little breakfast table
in the corner of her room.

She tells me,
"You don't have to come so much!"

"But I love talking to you,"
I say.

She makes me feel
at home—

more at home
than my real home.

I know it sounds weird but
I'd stay with her if I could.

Like every time I visit

I ask,
"Can you tell me
another story?"

READING TERMINAL MARKET

Me and this girl,
we'd look at each other
every day at the same Mediterranean food stand.
We started ordering the same salad and hummus
as our kind of secret language.

We invented languages back then
to say what we felt.

One day she sat closer to me.
She had short buzzed hair
and a tattoo behind her ear.

People didn't have as many tattoos back then,
so it was really unique.

One day I decided to take the leap
and I bought her food for her.

She thanked me and she went home with me—
told me she had wanted me for so long.

We cried that it had taken months
for us to talk.

She kissed me
and I kissed her

and the wait
ended up
being worth it.

GIRLS WHO LIKE GIRLS

Even though LGBTQIA2+ rights
have come a really long way,
it's frustrating how
we still have
like the same struggles
as decades ago.

Like, I've been
into so many girls
and we share looks
but I'm always too scared
to say anything—

it's exactly like
the story Lena just told.

ADVICE

I decide I want to ask Lena
for advice about Sophia and Pen.
I figure it couldn't hurt
and she has more experience
dating girls than anyone I know.

In school, we had health class last year
and there was a three-day unit on sex
where we just talked about STDs and contraception.
Why didn't we talk more about dating?

I'm not even talking about just queer dating,
like I don't think anyone learns about
how to have a relationship.

I know there's not just "one way"
but I feel like I have absolutely no clue
what I'm even doing.

How do I tell someone I like them a lot
without being creepy? How can I like
make conversations about consent be
open and actually helpful?

Why didn't anyone help me learn this???

I'm thinking about
how many queer people don't know someone
like Lena who they could even think of asking.

I TELL LENA

"So . . . so I want some advice maybe . . ."

"About?" Lena asks, even though
I can tell by her tone that she knows
it's about a girl.

Lena kind of knows everything
before it's going to happen.

I sigh.
"Actually . . . it's kind of about two girls . . ."

TWO GIRLS

I don't mean to like
    two girls at once.

I feel guilty.
    Isn't one girl enough?

        I don't even know
    what that means

to like
    two girls.

            I just don't know
    what I should do.

        Just feel
all mixed up.

    How can
        I like two girls

when I've never even
        dated   one?

TALKING ABOUT PEN AND SOPHIA

Lena listens and nods.
Then I tell her all about my date with Pen
and her eyes get wide.
I don't go into too many details because
that would feel super weird. But I do tell her
Pen and I have had sex.
I'm so thankful to have someone
to confide in. It takes me forever to tell her the whole thing
because I whisper (considering this is where I work)
and Lena can't hear super well,
so I say something and Lena goes, "Can you
say that again?" and then I say it louder
and get shy and then I lower my voice again
and it goes on and on. I tell Lena,
"Thank you for being so patient—
I know this is annoying—
me going on about it."

She waves her hand.
"Please! This is the most excitement
I've had for weeks."

WHAT TO DO

"That's certainly hard,"
Lena says. She ponders for a moment.

"Have you ever talked about how you feel
with Sophia?"

"No,"
I admit.

"Does she know you're interested in women?"

"Yeah, but only recently."

"Okay, well maybe you should make it a conversation.
All is easier said than done, but at some point, you have
to say
how you feel even if it doesn't go somewhere.
You need to
put it out there."

I nod. It makes sense
and I do trust her
but I don't know anyone
who talks that directly,
you know?

No one I know
just outright says,
"Hey I have feelings for you."

"And Pen?"
I ask.

      "You don't have to want to date Sophia
      to tell her how you feel.
      Maybe you just need closure—a way of finding an ending.
      There's certainly people I still think about
      because I never got that."

"That sounds hard."

      "You learn to cope."

      She looks around
      and I wonder what stories
      she's remembering.

      She adds, "You learn to relish
      the good times."

ODE TO WALKING

I walk home today
 and instead of taking the short route,
  I pace up and down the rows of houses.

I don't realize how long
 I've been walking
  till I check my phone and see

it's been about forty-five minutes,
 so I start to head back.
  It's hot but the sun is starting to set.

It reminds me of driving off alone
 with you, Lars, and I feel
  alive and free,

just like how I felt driving.
 The ground under my shoes
  is like how while driving you, Lars,

I felt every bump in the road.
 I know this is suburbia and not
  some national park or something

but I feel like the world is real.
 I told myself I wasn't going to check my messages
  the whole walk.

I raise my hands above my head to stretch.
 I can't believe June
  is almost over.

I get home and Mom looks surprised.
 I gloat a little bit
  about walking all the way home.

I LET MYSELF CHECK MY MESSAGES AND I HAVE:

Three missed calls and
Twenty-five text messages!!!

THE ONE TIME I DON'T CHECK MY PHONE

Sophia calls me and Pen texts me
and they both don't stop.

From a glance, it seems like

1) Sophia and Theo had a fight
and she's upset.
I can't quite
tell what it's about
but she wants
to meet up as soon as I can.
I hover on that notification
for a second. I think . . .
where were you
all these weeks?
Am I only useful
when she's fighting
with her boyfriend?????

2) Then, Pen texts that she wants to
"define" our relationship and I realize
I probably should have talked to her about that.

When do people usually talk
about what a relationship means with each other?

I'm also thinking,
how could both these people decide
they needed to talk at once?!

It makes me feel a little nervous / paranoid.
Do they know each other?

No, that's silly.

I think I just feel paranoid
because I do kind of still feel bad
for liking them both.

It kind of feels like
I'm cheating on them both?

But you know . . . I'm not dating either of them,
so it's not like
that's possible . . . right?

I WANT TO TURN OFF MY PHONE

and drive away—drive somewhere else
and start a new life with just you, Lars.
But, Lars, you're not

a real person and you're not even
a real car anymore. I want to
learn to let go of you—but I don't know how

when there's still so much that I miss.
I know it sounds dramatic to want to run away
because of all this

but it's always where my mind goes
when anything seems tough—
what does that say about me?

I wanted to run away from the car wreck
as soon as I saw the other driver was all right.
I wanted to just escape. How come

I'm so freaking bad at walking through
any tension? Why can't I just tell people
how I feel and who I am?

What if I never find the courage to?

CLASSROOM DEBATE

Last year in English class,
we were learning about writing
persuasive essays
and we ended the unit
with a class-wide debate.

The subject was "school uniforms"
and we had to each
take a stance.

In writing, I had no problem explaining
why I thought school uniforms sucked.

We picked three argument points:

1) Uniforms don't let people express themselves.

2) Uniforms might punish or limit queer people's gender
expressions.

3) It's extra work to police uniforms
and will probably make some students
feel bad about themselves.

But when the class debate came,
I like was so shaky
and nervous I could barely
get a word in and it was
my team's turn to talk.

When I was writing, it felt less like arguing
and more like explaining an idea.

I was so mad at myself.
Why did I avoid conflict
so much in person?

I guess I hated the idea
of anyone being upset with me
when the debate was over.

Something I've been thinking about, though,
is that avoiding conflict and tension
might not be a good thing
like I usually think it is.

Like if I did actually run away
and never texted Sophia or Pen back,
that would mean
none of us would ever talk about anything.

I have to call Sophia,
even if I don't get the courage this time
to tell her
it's hard for me
to listen to her talk about Theo
because really
I wish I was with her.

I have to text Pen
even if I'm not sure
how I'd even want to define
our relationship yet.

ADVICE?

I wish I had parents
who I could ask
for advice.

Does anyone ask
their parents for advice
on things like this?

Did Mom ever feel
like she had no one to turn to?
Did Dad?

I CALL SOPHIA

I go to my room and ask Chris if I can just have a few minutes
alone there. He groans but walks out. For a minute, I think about
how if I just I had my own room, I might feel less like a constant
tornado of emotions. I call Sophia and listen to her talk for what
seems like hours but is only really like twenty minutes. She just
monologues about some stuff between her and Theo. Honestly, I
kind of zone in and out which is a shitty thing for a friend to do
but . . . here we are.

Basically, it boils down to Theo not wanting to actually date
her and her thinking they were a couple and not just into each
other. I try to humor her even though I don't see how it matters.
They've only really started hanging out the last few weeks. I
know it's selfish but I keep thinking about how she hasn't really
asked me how I've been during this phone call. I know I should
tell her I want to talk about me a little, but I don't. I just listen
and listen and listen and listen and listen.

She keeps circling back to Theo. It hurts more and more. I start
to hang on to some other details she shares about Theo. She says,
"He like takes my phone sometimes just to leave me little love
notes, he says—but then he'll be on my social media pages and
email and stuff." Then, "Sometimes he'll call me in the middle
of the night to wake me up and check on me." I'm thinking . . .
what the fuck? That's kind of gross—seems creepy if you ask me.
Am I allowed to tell her that? Should I ask her how it makes her
feel? I don't want her to think I'm just saying that because I like
her. Does she even know I like her?

Finally, I just say, "He seems like . . . a full-time job haha." She
gets upset and says, "He just cares about me actually." I can't

tell if the comment is pointed at me but it definitely feels like it. What did I do wrong? All I've done is be there for her. I lie and say I was just kidding and she eases up and admits, "Yeah . . . it kind of is a full-time job."

As she winds down her venting session about Theo, I think about what Lena said about being honest. I know next time I see Sophia I'm going to have to tell her. We're still going to meet up Saturday.

I lie on my bed and look up at the ceiling before picking up my phone again.

I TEXT PEN

ME: Hey! I'm sorry I didn't see this till now!

ME: Do you want to talk soon?

PEN: Can we just do it over text?

I really don't want to
talk about our relationship
over text.

I like to be in front of a person
for anything serious but I know

Pen gets nervous about that.

Everyone communicates differently.
Ugh, I hate this.

ME: Okay, maybe we could talk about it later then?

ME: After we text?

PEN: Okay!

ME: So, what are you thinking?

PEN: I'm thinking I'm not sure if I want to date anyone right now.

PEN: I like you a lot but I like—I don't think I want to date

ME: Oh okay, thanks for letting me know.

PEN: Are you mad?

ME: Do you mean date like go on dates
or do you mean
like partner / girlfriend stuff?

The other problem with "dating"
is like every term could have
800 meanings. To some people, "dating"
is like casual, and other people
have been "dating" for a year.
What does it even mean???

PEN: I just don't want partner / girlfriend stuff.

PEN: I like hanging out with you!

PEN: I want to keep seeing you just not with a label right now.

I don't know why this hurts my feelings
when it's exactly what I want too?

I guess no matter what
we all have been kind of taught
we're supposed to want a partner.

ME: Yeah I get that.

PEN: You understand?

ME: Totally.

ME: Maybe we could hang out this coming weekend? Saturday?

PEN: That sounds great I'm free!

Then, I want to ask her
why she doesn't want
to have a relationship with me . . .

Is she interested in someone else?

Did I do something wrong?

Is it something ABOUT me?

Am I too awkward?

Not good enough at makeup?

Don't listen to enough cool bands?

Ugh—I hate wondering . . .

PEOPLE ARE STRESSFUL

I spend the rest of the night wondering
why Pen doesn't want to date me.

I kind of wish
she wouldn't have even
brought it up

which I know is bad. I should be glad
she's telling me exactly
how she feels.

I am likeable, aren't I, Lars?

I feel like I'm not good enough or something
but I remind myself
I didn't really want a girlfriend
anyway.

In the depths of all my thoughts spiraling,
I start wondering if I could like some more boys
if I really tried.

After all, I am bisexual
and I do like some boys,
just not really anyone
in my life right now.

It's hard because
for me I feel like I really have to know someone
to actually really like them.

I know that's not how it works—
I can't just decide I'm going to ignore
how I feel about Sophia and Pen—

there's still just sometimes this voice
that tells me all this stress
is my fault.
Sophia doesn't even notice
I like her, and Pen
doesn't want to date me.

Maybe I'm not cut out for dating. Maybe
I'm not cut out
for dating girls.

I keep thinking
of any other reasons
I can blame this on.

Maybe it's because
Pen's only out to her family.
Maybe it's that. Sigh,
but probably
not.

IN THE MIDST OF ALL THIS WHIRLING

I realize I asked
both Pen and Sophia
to hang out

on Saturday.

Why did I do that?

It's my only day off and now I'm going
to stress the whole rest of the week.

No. No.

I'm not going to freak out, Lars.

I'm just going to plan to hang out
at different times.

Yeah—that could work.

I want to walk back to the nursing home
and talk to Lena but I don't want
to make her feel like
she has to be my therapist or something.

I guess I just wish there were
even just like one movie I could think of
with a happy lesbian relationship
that doesn't end tragically
or super sad.

I know fiction
isn't reality but maybe it could help me
figure some of this out.

CHRIS KNOCKS

I sit up in bed. "Hey,"
I say even though I don't really
want to talk right now.

I kind of wish
he didn't want
to come back in the room.

      "What's up?" he asks.
      He sounds hesitant.

"Oh, you know,
normal-level drama."

      "Ah, I see."
      He pauses and walks over
      to shut our door. It clicks closed.

      "Can I ask you something?"

"Hmm?"

      "What would you think
      if we came out together?
      Like, the both of us."

"Came out?
Like as queer?"
I ask.

I'm not entirely sure
what he means by "together."

      "Yeah, maybe this summer.
      We have lots of time to think about
      how to do it."

My impulse is to tell him
he's crazy but I don't
want to hurt his feelings
so, I pause.

"Why?"
I ask.

There has to be
some reason
he feels like
he's in
such a hurry.

"Why?"

"Yeah, why now?"

> "I want them to know. I feel like
> I'm holding something in—
> like I'm always lying."

"Yeah, that's kinda how it is,"
I say. I can't believe
Chris wants to tell our parents.
Things are tense enough lately!

I don't need them to have
another reason not to trust me.
No thank you!

> "I think they might come around,"
> Chris says, full of hope.

I'm thinking
there has to be something else
going on—
Chris can't have just decided
he wants to endure
telling Mom and Dad.

"It's true they might,"
I say, after a too-long pause.
I don't know how to tell him
that I don't want to do it
together . . . I honestly feel like
Mom and Dad would accept Chris
before they'd accept me.

"Can I just help you come out?"
I ask. I don't get why I
have to be part of this.

"You don't want to tell them?"
Chris asks.

He seems a little annoyed???

Like . . . this is my choice;
if I NEVER told Mom and Dad,
it would still be my choice.

"I just like don't know if I'm ready.
I don't know if I ever want to.
We talked about this."

        "I just felt like doing it together might
        be easier," Chris says.

He's really sticking to this
isn't he?

I also think if we came out together,
Mom and Dad would think
I influenced Chris or something
because I'm the older sibling.
I definitely don't need
more points against me.

I'm trying to earn back their trust,
not burn it to the ground.

I have a whole other year of living here.
I just have to survive that.

"It might be . . ."
I say to try to close the discussion
without outright saying "no."

I love Chris for his positivity.
He sounds genuinely excited
about the idea of coming out.

Maybe I'm being too negative.

I ask,
"How would you want to do it?"

COMING OUT PRODUCTIONS

Chris pulls up this "coming out" YouTube video on his phone.
In the first cut, the girl in the video writes
"I'm Gay!" in big chalk letters
on her driveway for her parents to see
when they come home.

The next scene shows
her family hugging her and telling her they're
proud of her and everyone is crying and laughing.

It seems like a scene from a movie or something.

Are families actually this happy???

I don't think our family would ever react like that but
for a minute I want to pretend with Chris that they might.

Then, I do think of moments
when there have been a lot of joy.

For my tenth birthday,
Mom and Dad threw me
a chocolate-themed surprise party.

I was going through a phase
of wanting to be a baker
and Mom and Dad made a whole bunch
of little desserts. We had
a chocolate "sampling"
with just lots of candy bars.

It was wonderful. I guess they can
do stuff like that. They've just done less recently.

"It's like a promposal only with coming out," I say.
I try to smile—
try to imagine this kind of celebration
in our tiny apartment.

"Exactly!" Chris says.

"Would you do something
like this?"

"I don't know what yet but I want
to make a video!
I want it to be like a *production*."
Chris does jazz hands to accentuate
"production."

I laugh.
"Haha a production?"

Since Chris came out to me,
he's definitely let himself be a little more femme
and I love it for him.

He can love sports video games
and be more effeminate
and I love that about him.

"Yeah. I feel like if it's over-the-top enough,
Mom and Dad
would feel too bad being rude about it."

I think he does have a point there.
It's actually not the worst idea . . .

It's still hard for me to wrap my mind around.
We're just not people who do stuff like that.

Looking at the last few seconds of the video,
I also think that I guess I don't know
what this girl's family is like off camera either.

I CAN'T BELIEVE I MIGHT WANT TO DO THIS

A little bit after watching that video . . .
    I'm finding myself kind of wanting to do one . . . I think Chris
    might have actually almost convinced me that maybe we
    should try.
        Maybe if we do it together it will mean they can't disown
        us—they'd have to disown us both!
        What a messed-up thing to think at all . . .
            I guess I'm sure that's happened before but it does mean
            they'd have to see both of us at once? I hope I can do it.
            I think I'm more scared than Chris.
                Why? Maybe he's braver than me.

WE'RE BOTH SCROLLING ON OUR PHONES
ON EITHER SIDE OF THE ROOM

When I say,
"Okay . . . okay I will at least try
the whole coming-out thing . . ."

ODE / ANTI-ODE TO FUTURES

I don't know if everyone does this
but I can't help but think far into the future
for everything I do. In school I think,
"How will this get me a job?
        What kind of job?
                What will my house look like?
                    Will I make enough money to survive?"
In relationships I think,
"Could I spend my life with this person?
        What would our wedding look like?
             What would our family look like?
            Could we get old together?"

For my family I think,
"Will I make them proud?
    Will they accept me?
        Where will I go if they don't?
        Will they ever know me?"

AMBULANCES

I get to work and there's an ambulance in the parking lot.
There are always ambulances at the nursing home
and I'm always worried something's happened to Lena.

I walk quicker and look to see if I can recognize anyone
and I do. Macy, a woman on the third floor, lays on a stretcher.
She's shaking her fist, saying,
        "I'm completely fine!
        Just twisted my ankle is all!"

My supervisor for the day, a mom-aged lady with curly hair,
comes out front to tell me to move along
and not to stare. She tells me,
        "Everything is okay,
        move along now."

I WORRY IN CIRCLES

I worry

in circles and   the worries

never leave   my head.

New worries about   Lena getting sick

replace the worries   about Pen and Sophia.

It's like a worry spiral.   This worry for that worry.

I do my usual   duties of making food

for the residents and   delivering fresh towels

and bringing snacks   to everyone's rooms,

my brain   spinning

all day.

JOAN'S DAUGHTER

Joan Alba is always
the first person I visit on my rounds.
Her room is at the front of the building
on the memory-loss floor.

At first, that place used to make me nervous.
It scared me to think about forgetting
parts of my life.
I worried about knowing what to do
if they were scared or confused
and sometimes they are,
but they're also happy sometimes
and caring and thoughtful just like anyone
without dementia.

Joan sometimes thinks I'm her daughter
and sometimes she thinks I'm an old friend.
I always just go along with what she says.
It makes her more comfortable
and besides, we have a lot of fun!
She'll tell me inside jokes I don't know
and I'll laugh like I understand and she'll laugh too.

I know it sounds weird
but I wish I lived here sometimes,
even when it's a rough day
like last week when Joan
was crying and didn't know why.
I held her hand and she held mine.
I said, "We'll be okay."

>   She said, "You're right,
>   we will be."

MOMS

Like usual, after work I visit Lena.
She has new flowers on her side table.
I ask, "Who are those from?"
and then I add, "Oh! I'm sorry,
I don't mean to like be nosy."

>   Lena laughs
>   and says she doesn't mind.
>   She winks and says,
>   "They're from
>   a lady I'm chatting with."

"Lena! You're KIDDING!
From the dating app?"
I ask.

"You bet!"
She winks.

I can't believe
there are two eighty-year-old lesbians
in my tiny conservative town.

The flowers are purple and bright.

I say, "Oh my gosh
you have to tell me what she's like."

>Lena says
>"Her name is Marie
>and she still lives on her own
>with a little house and a little garden."

She shows me a picture on her phone
of a bright lush garden
full of ripe strawberries
and winding cherry tomato plants.
Is this the Garden of Eden?

"Oh my gosh that is
THE BEST!"

She shows me another picture—
this one is of Marie.
She has very short, curly white hair.
She's wearing shimmery pink lipstick
with little gold-and-pearl earrings
that look beautiful against her brown skin.

>"She came out at fifty-five
>and never met anyone yet,"
>Lena says.
>"I can't believe my luck."
>She chuckles.

"Wow . . . she sounds
really interesting!"
I say.

       Lena sighs and says,
       "Sometimes I wonder if
       my mom was like that—
       just never had the language
       to explain it."

"You think your mom was gay?"
I ask, before I realize
that sounds a little blunt.

       "I can't be sure but
       I do think it was possible.
       She left her husband, my daddy,
       when I was little.
       She always had a close girlfriend.
       I don't think any of them actually dated
       but maybe in a different world they might have . . .
       It's hard, you never really know.

       Sometimes, I think I dream
       it for myself . . . as a way to explain
       her not accepting me."

"I get that . . . yeah you never know . . ."
I say. I feel sad.
I wish I was better at knowing
what to say to about stuff like this.

       "Do you wonder about your mom?"
       Lena asks.

I laugh and tell her
"I'm sure MY mom isn't."

       Lena asks
       "What makes you so sure?"

and I realize I guess I really can't be sure.
I don't know what everyone else is thinking.

I ask her how well she knew her mom
and Lena says they stopped talking
when she came out.

I feel so sad for her even though she waves her hand
and tells me not to feel bad.

Lena says, "I've made my peace with this."

I can't imagine being able to
move on from that
but I guess she had to—was forced to.

INVITATION

Before I leave,
Lena invites me to
the senior talent show
this Saturday.

She says, "I understand if you're busy
but I'd love for you to come."

I can't think of anything
I'd like to do more.

She laughs and tells me
that she's going to sing.

She says, "I used to sing all the time—
I was in an all girls chorus
in college. I've kept up with it
on my own. I'm excited
to share it."

I didn't even know
Lena sang.

I try to picture her—
just a little older than me
in rows and rows of girls
spilling songs into the air.

> "It was a kind of unofficial
> lesbian chorus," she says with a wink.

"Ha! I want to be in a lesbian chorus—
but yeah
of course, I'll be there!"

Why do I do this, Lars?

I can't even lie and say
I forgot I was going to meet up with
Sophia and Pen.

I was just enjoying being with Lena so much
and I don't want to say no to her.

She's had so many people
say "no" to her,
from her family to
the girls she's loved
and who didn't love her back.

I want to be there for her.
I feel lucky to have her
as my friend.

I guess part of it is also
I really, I hate saying no
to anyone.

If I could never have to say "no,"
I never would.

I hate feeling like
I let anyone
down.

I DON'T KNOW WHAT I'LL TELL PEN AND SOPHIA

Saying yes to everything
   doesn't
      ever
         work.

Maybe I should just cancel on them . . .
   But it's my only day off
      and I haven't seen them recently
         and I want to see them both!

Maybe I should just tell Lena I can't . . .
   But it means a lot to her
      and it sounds like fun . . .
         more fun than being stressed
            hanging out
               with Sophia and Pen . . .

LARS, WHAT WOULD YOU DO?

I know. I know.
You're a car—
a car that isn't a car anymore.

But I also feel like
you had a bold spirit.

When I drove you,
I felt
like I trusted myself.

I felt like I could
be myself
and make my own decisions.

So, I'm asking you,

what would you do?

Well, I guess you probably
wouldn't get yourself
into a position like this.

But how would you solve it?
I'm getting this image of us driving
and picking both Sophia and Pen up.

I feel like
I'm having a séance
for a car . . .

but maybe that's not
the worst idea.

Ha! Maybe I should invite them!

Not sure how they'd feel about
spending a Saturday afternoon
at a nursing home.

I've told both of them about Lena though,
and they both think she sounds
super cool.

Maybe this could work.

DIFFERENT WORLDS

Sometimes I feel like

     I have a different version of myself

       for every person I know.

  It's not that I'm lying.   I just notice myself change.

I wonder if there's one real me

      somewhere between all of them.

With Lena I feel   closest to being myself.

    I feel like my parents have   no idea who I am anymore.

I act how they'd want me to act   because I'm scared if I don't,

       they won't love me like they did.

Does everyone feel like this?   I think being queer

   can sometimes make me feel fractured.

I feel in between everything.   I know I'm queer

   but there's not a core place
       where I feel at home.

BAD DECISION I

I know the first bad decision was saying "yes"
to too many things this weekend.

But, that I could have easily
recovered from.

BAD DECISION II

I was texting

Sophia   and Pen

at once. I was trying

to figure out   what to do

about Saturday and next thing I knew,

I was asking   Sophia

if she wanted   to come and then

I was asking Pen   and then I realized I

didn't want to tell   either one

that the other   was coming

and that's not   a good sign at all.

I asked Pen   if it could be a date

and she said "yes,"   and I asked Sophia

for a friend's day out   and she said "yes,"

and it can't really   be both of those

at once. I just didn't want

either of them   to say no.

BAD DECISION III

I pace my room.
What am I going to do?

This is like a textbook
teen catastrophe
that I lead myself into.

I blame you, Lars!
You talked me into this.

I was just like
yes—I can make everyone happy.

That's not true!

When has that ever
been true?

I really do want
to see Pen and Sophia
and Lena on Saturday.

I have a whole summer, though.

Why did I have to squeeze
this all into one day?

Maybe . . . maybe I should just
tell them both that the other is coming?

That way it's like clear.
After all, Sophia is my friend
and no one knows
I like her.

It could just be
three of us hanging out.

That could work.

Of course that would work.

I start a group chat
with all of us
and I text:

Saturday is going to be fun with all of us together!
You guys are going to love Lena!

REGRETS . . .

Sigh
There were probably more tactful ways to do this—
I know. I guess I hoped
Pen and Sophia
would just go along with it
and the anxiety spiral
would finally
be over.

Lately, I feel like
I'm always in a new whirlwind.

It's not really that weird.
Is it?

We're just all going to hang out.
My best friend
and my new friend.

I guess really
I should have just rescheduled
but instead, I'm here
trying to jam everything into one night.

I was trying to make everyone happy
but this isn't even what
anyone wanted.

I pace the house, nervous to read their reactions.

How could I make such a mess
of such normal interactions?

God, I should have just
been honest about it all.

I was so worried about upsetting someone
and I probably upset both of them.
I can't blame this on you, Lars.
It was just

all me.

PART 3

Odes to Myself as a Future Old Bisexual

WHAT'S WRONG WITH ME?

I lie sometimes.
Like, I blatantly lie.
I don't think I'm a compulsive liar—
it's more like I let myself say things
I don't mean, which is messed up—
so that I don't have to
let people down.

It's kind of manipulative, I think
(is that the right word?)
and I want to stop.

I'm making a pact with myself
to not do crappy stuff like this again.

I just need to be honest with people
I care about.

I have to trust them
to love me
even if I make mistakes.

SOPHIA: I don't know Pen so I'd feel kinda weird, you know?

SOPHIA: I just don't want to be a third wheel and ruin your time.

SOPHIA: Maybe we could just pick another day?

ME: Yeah totally! I'm sorry I thought it would be nice if you guys met.

(I did not want them to meet.)

SOPHIA: Yeah maybe someday.

SOPHIA: I just want to talk to you first.

(What does that mean???)

ME: Yeah maybe after work on Monday?

SOPHIA: Sure!

PEN: Oh that sounds interesting.

PEN: I don't know if I want to hang out with Sophia though.

PEN: Not because I don't like her.

PEN: You just have known each other forever and I feel like I'd be like awk

PEN: Okay so I just have to ask this

PEN: Did you guys have a thing?

ME: No no no haha we're just friends!

PEN: Didn't she kind of ditch you for a guy?

PEN: You were telling me

PEN: I'm sorry I'm not trying to bring stuff up that's not my business

ME: Yeah . . . yeah kinda.

PEN: How long is this . . . senior talent show?

PEN: Will anyone like our age be there?

PEN: Ugh I'm sorry that was an asshole thing to ask

PEN: Why don't we just pick another day

ME: Okay!

PEN: I'm free that Sunday

ME: Okay we could like go after work then
I get off at like 8pm

PEN: Let's do that—that's late for you right haha?

ME: Ha! Yes . . .

THERE ARE FEW THINGS MORE BEAUTIFUL THAN CANCELED PLANS

I feel so relieved
even though I also feel
kinda bad.
I basically ditched
Sophia and Pen
for this old lady I met
a few weeks ago.

But she's not just an old lady,
she's my friend.

Why don't we make friends
with people of different ages?

I guess really
I just feel bad
that I just tried
to make everyone happy
and that ended up mixing everything up.

I wish I wouldn't have tried
to date anyone this summer.

I wish I had you, Lars, to carry me
out down the highway
and through the cornfields

when I needed to get away.
It's not that I don't like Pen—
it's just really hard.

I keep dreaming of just
living alone forever.

Maybe I'll end up
like Lena. It doesn't seem
so bad. She's not alone—
she has her own space.

She reads all the time
and works on her art.
I could survive like that.
Haha and she even has
a baby gay (haha me!)
as a friend.

Maybe I could
like create a house
for queer kids
to feel safe. We could visit
older queer people
and talk to each other
and learn about
all the different ways
to be a queer person.

ODE TO MYSELF AS A FUTURE OLD BISEXUAL

I hope I have short gray hair
and a bandana tied around my head.
I hope I wear jean shorts
and that I have a flower garden
and a strawberry patch and I just

relax and watch old movies all day.
Maybe I could start a book swap on my porch.
I don't even care if I have
a partner—I just want to be my bold queer self
and not feel worried about
trying to explain it to anyone.
I hope I'm at least a little like Lena.

COMING-OUT VIDEOS

Almost every night now,
Chris and I share coming-out videos with each other
for ideas.

All the videos end happily
and they're really encouraging to us.

One night, Chris asks
if I think there are other coming-out videos
that were destroyed
because people's friends
or parents or community
reacted negatively.

I say, "I'm not sure,"
even though we both know
there probably are videos like that.

> "Promise we'll keep the video
> even if Mom and Dad
> react like that—like not happy for us,"
> he says.

I want to say "no"
but I have to be strong for him.

I don't think I've ever felt
more like an older sibling than now.

He is so bright
and so vibrant.

I want this to be easy for him.

I wish I could know everything will turn out okay.

We still haven't figured out
a way to tell our story but it will come,

I know it.

I say,
"Yes, we'll keep the video."

HAIRCUTS

Sometimes, Mom decides she wants to do
Chris's and my hair
on her day off.

I don't get it because it's her day to NOT do hair
and usually, she has a specific plan
for what she wants to do with us.

I guess she does have a lot more days off now,
with less hours at the salon.

I always want to ask
why she doesn't look
for work at other places or maybe try
a new salon.

I know it's not that easy.

I guess I just feel like it's not fair
for things to be harder now
than when I was younger.

That's not how
it's supposed to work.

But somehow
that's the way

life is.

MOM'S HAIRCUTS

Always look nice
but they're like never quite my style.

It's Friday, the day before Lena's show,
and it's early.

      At breakfast,
Mom is already talking about doing our hair.

She's off today because she has to work Saturday.
She touches Chris's shaggy pile of curls.
      "What if we gave you something fresh?
      More summery?" she says.

  Chris says, "It's fine, I like it the way it is."

      "No, no I have an idea!" Mom says.

Chris shoots me a desperate look.

  "I like it like this," Chris says.

      "No, no you have to see what I have planned.
      I'll get you, too, Claire, while I'm at it."

"Can I choose it?"

Mom pauses a second.
I almost never
have an opinion about my hair.

It's been medium length
for years. It's been curled and in a bob
and dyed a few different "normal" colors.

When I was younger,
it was fun to see what style
my mom would come up with
but now I kind of want
to have my own style—

like how Pen has her own style.

> "Oh . . . I mean sure.
> What do you have in mind?"
> Mom says.

BUTCH

I've never thought of myself as any gender other than a girl
but I have always been curious about girls who play with gender
expression.

Lately, I've been Googling pictures of girls with
super short hair. I love all the styles. Sometimes boyish,

sometimes more like a pixie. Sometimes drastic shaved sides.
I want a haircut with energy. Can a haircut be queer?

Maybe it's just that a haircut could make a queer person feel
more visible.
I don't think about any of this when I show my mom a picture

of a very butch woman with short hair as the reference
for how I want my hair to look. Mom looks concerned.

She takes the phone from my hand. In that moment I realize
she might associate the haircut with being a lesbian or
something.

I don't know what to say. I fumble, "I have a friend who cut her
hair short
and she says it's super easy to take care of!"

It seems too late.

WATCHING CHRIS GET HIS HAIRCUT

Mom always just gives us haircuts
in the kitchen. She leans a kitchen chair up to the sink
to wash it first. When I was younger,
I was jealous of other kids who got to go to salons.
I knew my mom worked at one but the chairs seemed so cool.
Mom took us to her salon once to show us it was basically
the same thing. She works the shampoo into his hair.
She scolds him for not washing it better on his own.
Mom always says you should wash hair twice
to make sure it's clean. Chris groans.
He tells her not to cut it too short.
There are no mirrors in our kitchen so you can never really see
what Mom is doing. Little wet snippets of his brown hair
fall to the floor. I can tell it's shorter than he wanted.
Chris likes his hair. Maybe he even wants to grow it out.
I want to tell her to stop but I know she wouldn't take it well.
In the living room, the TV is on
and there's a story about someone getting asked to leave a diner
because she was there with her girlfriend holding hands.
I listen and I want to just change the channel. I hate hearing that
in the background. Chris shares a look with me. I try to say
without words that I'll always have his back.

ODE TO MY HAIR

It's my turn now.

I savor mom washing my hair. As she does, I let my mind drift. I
think about driving in my car with all my windows down at the
beginning of the summer before the crash. I think of the wind in
my hair. I couldn't even hear the radio over the breeze. I reached
one hand out the window because I'd seen people do that. I
wished I could close my eyes but I had to watch the road. I could
feel every single follicle, like a cornfield planted all on my head.
I miss that car so much. It's such a dumb thing to miss. The

shampoo tingles at the roots as she scrubs. Mom is talking but I'm not hearing her. She repeats herself a few times.

"Claire? Claire? Hellooo? Sit up, you're all done."

I come back to reality.

"Were you daydreaming there?"

"Yeah actually."

Mom smiles. For a second, I feel bad for worrying that she might judge me for being queer. Maybe I'm making a big deal out of nothing but I know people can change when they know the truth. She dries my hair off with a pink towel and gets out her scissors.

GIRLS WITH SHORT HAIR

I've always thought of girls with short hair
as being free from something.

I know that hair means something different
to everyone. Everyone is always telling me

to grow my hair out longer—
that it would look so nice if I grew it out

just a little more. Maybe that's why
I think of short hair as free—free from

what other people want me to be.

"ARE YOU SURE?"

Mom asks, "Are you sure you want to go *this* short?"
She sounds sad and it makes me
want to take it back and say,
"No, just a trim."
I stay firm.
This is what I want.

It reminds me of how little
I talk to my mom anymore.
I'm scared once I come out, she won't like me.
Sometimes, I feel like she's
always judging me.
She's always wanted me
to achieve so much.
She wants
only the best grades.
Only the best work.
Never in trouble.
Never making
any mistakes.
It's hard to live up to sometimes,
so I just push her away.
I know she loves me.
I wish she said it more often.
I show her a picture on my phone
of a punkish pixie cut.
    "Is this a famous person?" She asks, genuinely curious.
I laugh because I don't know who it is.
I just found the picture searching Google Images
for the right haircut.
"Haha, no, Mom, I just liked the cut."
    "Oh okay."
She sets to work.
Why did I think
she'd say "no"?
I feel like maybe
this is progress.

CLUB SANDWICHES

When Chris was still in day care, sometimes mom would pick
just me up on half days at school. I felt so lucky to be the older
sibling. We would stop at the diner up the street. Mom always

got a turkey club sandwich. She'd let me have the little colorful toothpicks that held the stacked sandwiches together and her spears of pickle. One day, I asked if I could order my own. She warned me I might not finish it but I did. From then on, we ordered the same thing each time and stacked our toothpicks in between us. We haven't gone for years though. I miss that.

Maybe we could get back to that place.

NEW HAIRCUT

Mom sighs and stands back.
   "Will you ever grow it out again?"

"Let me see!" I say.

I get up and walk to the bathroom
to look in the mirror.

It's so short. I have to touch it
so it feels real. I run a hand through it.
It's exactly like the picture!

   "Do you like it?" she asks.

"I love it!"

   "Sometimes a change is good,"
   she says a little hesitantly.

I feel embarrassed
by all her attention

and the short hair
does make me feel

vulnerable—like I don't blend in anymore.
I know plenty of people have short hair,

it's just new to me.

"Thank you so much, Mom."

   "It's no problem, just promise me you're not
   joining a punk band
   or a protest or something."

I know Mom is just teasing
but the comment still makes me sad.

I tell myself at least she didn't say
the haircut makes me look

"like a lesbian" or something.

Would it be so bad
if she thought that, though?

I kind of do
want to look

like a queer girl
but there's not one way

to look like a queer girl.

I kind of hope
the haircut helps her see me.

THIS HAIRCUT MAKES ME LOOK BUTCH AND I LOVE IT

I feel like a sentence changes meaning
based on who says it.

I was so scared Mom or Dad would tell me
that I look "gay" with my new haircut

but when I say it to myself,
I feel powerful.

ODE TO WALKING WITH MY BROTHER

Car rides are a great place to talk
but walks give you so much more time.

Forgive me, Lars,
but I do think

I'm starting to find places
to be myself without you.

       Chris asks, "Do you miss driving?"

as we walk
to the nursing home.

I convinced him to go with me
to Lena's talent show. I have been

telling him about her lately.
I tell him,

"I think I might be
happy I don't have the car, actually.
It's made me take up space again
in our house, with our parents.
It's made me see the town differently.
At first, I felt trapped and now I feel curious."

I admit, "Haha, it would make dates easier though."

       Chris says, "I do think
       I want to buy a car."

I ask, "Why?
It's sooo expensive."

       He says,
       "Haha a getaway car."

"For what though?" I ask.

"I mean I know
there's a million things
but anything specific?"

> "I don't know.
> I'm like going crazy.
> Every day I feel like trapped
> in school
> and this town."

> He pauses, stopping on a corner
> before crossing the street.
> "I guess I just want to experience
> getting away a little."

"We'll find ways out,
we will," I tell him,
even though I ask myself
the same questions.

SENIOR TALENT SHOW

When Chris and I get there,
I'm surprised to see

Sophia is waiting outside!!!

She's standing on the sidewalk
in a nice blue flowery summer dress
with matching sapphire eyeliner.

That's not usual for her.
I mean Sophia always looks nice
but she doesn't usually wear
vibrant eyeliners and stuff.

I also wasn't expecting her so, at first,
I don't even fully register that this is Sophia.

She waves and Chris elbows me.
"How did you get here?" I ask.
I feel a tug of excitement.
Sophia? Surprising me?

>"I figured I didn't have anything better to do,"
>she says. "Plus I've been curious
>about Lena since you've been
>telling me about her."

"Aw you should have texted me,
I would have dressed nice,"
I say, gesturing
to her dress.

>"I love your hair—
>you didn't tell me you got it cut,"
>she says.

"My mom actually just
did it yesterday."

>"Can I touch it?" she asks.

My heart leaps.

Of course, I want her to touch me
but I'm scared.

She means so much to me
and I felt like

I was just starting
to get more levelheaded
about her.

I wonder if
she'll ever feel

the way I do.

"Yeah," I say,
laughing a little,
"You can touch it."

She does,
running her hands
through it.

"Oooh soft," she says.

I try my hardest
not to blush.

I remember Chris is there too.

I glance at him
and he raises an eyebrow.

Awkward!

Sophia knows Chris
because she's come over for playdates
since we were kids.

We all make small talk together
before going in
and finding seats
in the common area.

Some of my coworkers
say hello and tease me
for coming
in on a day off.

THE SHOW SO FAR

There's a man who tells really absurd jokes.
One goes like this,
"Why did the chicken cross the road?
He was out of bran!"

Everyone laughs
Sometimes he can't read his notes,
so he just says,
            "Eh, forget that one."

There's two women
who play triangles
with different rhythms

and one woman
who does an interpretive dance
only in arm gestures.

These people are fabulous.

It makes me think
about the stories they all have.

I want to talk to them all.

Each performer
is more wonderful
than the next.

Chris and Sophia
seem to be having a great time.

Sophia touches my arm
in the middle of a song a couple is singing
and whispers,

    "This is so fun! I can't believe
    I almost missed it!"

HOT / COLD

Is this the same person
who, just a week or so ago,

ditched me to hang out
with Theo???

Sure, I'm loving this.
I just don't understand

what's going on.
I mean, I know what's going on.

Theo is probably busy tonight
and she probably has nothing else to do.

A part of me feels hurt.
Another part of me says

I should just be happy
to have this time with her.

I keep wondering,
how did Sophia decide

to hang out with me?
Does she really want to be here

with me

or is she just
bored?

LENA PERFORMS

She sings a song she wrote.
She hadn't told me exactly what
her act was going to be.

Her voice is gruff but soft.
She plays the old, slightly out-of-tune piano.
She sings about a girl she loved
decades ago. The chorus goes

I miss her fingers through my hair.
I wake up and she's not there.
I wake up and she's gone away.
I wake up and she's a windowsill.

I feel this impulse
to grab Sophia's hand.

I shake it off
and rest my hands on my lap.

I want to love someone
like the girls in Lena's memories.

ODE TO SOPHIA'S VOICE

Hearing Lena sing
makes me think of Sophia's voice.

They kind of have
opposite voices.

Lena's is soft like curtains
and Sophia's is strong and bold

and swelling like waves.

Last year, the chorus sang a *Les Miserables* medley
and she sang a solo for "On My Own."

I also missed the next line of music
after her solo was over,

my breath was so taken away.

Then I imagine Sophia
singing the song Lena sang.

Just the thought
melts me.

What would it feel like
for her to sing to me?

Why am I torturing myself
with something

that isn't going
to happen?

AFTER THE SHOW

I go up first to hug Lena.
　　　She says, half teasing, "Why on earth
　　　would you come to work when you're off?"

I say, "I came to see you!
It was amazing!"

　　　She says, "I just would think
　　　you kids had something better to do."
　　　She's still teasing.

"One: This is literally the best show in town.
Two: We are not especially interesting,"
I say.

　　　Lena laughs and says,
　　　"No that's not true."

I give her a hug
and she smells like lavender
as always.

I want to tell her I'm so happy
we're friends but I don't know
if she thinks of us as friends.

Lena glances over at Sophia
and raises her eyebrows at me.

I whisper,
"She's just my friend,
Stop!"

I'm sooooo worried
Sophia saw this exchange
but she seems kind of oblivious,

taking in the home's decor.
"I'll tell you more later,"
I say to Lena.

She squeezes my hand.

SHE'S JUST MY FRIEND

She's just my friend.
She's just my friend.
She's just my friend.
She's just my friend.
She's just my friend.
She's just my friend.
She's just my friend.
She's just my friend.
She's just my friend.
She's just my friend.
She's just my friend
   even though
   I know I have feelings for her.

   Even though
   I think about her every day.

   Even though
   I can't imagine being with anyone else
     in the same way.

I'M GOING TO STOP SEEING PEN

I know we're not even
  really *dating*.

I just think it's not fair to her
  if I feel this strongly about Sophia.

Maybe she wouldn't mind
     that I'm into Sophia.

I wish there were more people to talk to
     about things like this.

Even on TV, I feel like I've never seen
     a girl like me with problems like this.

Ha, Lena would tell me
     I should write about it or make a painting
                 or a song.

Maybe I will . . .

A POEM FOR SOPHIA THAT SHE WILL NEVER SEE

Dear Sophia,

Did you start
wearing a new perfume this summer?
Or is it a new body wash?
A shampoo?
I always prefer scrubs—
that feeling of grit
across skin.

I want to tell you that I've noticed
but it seems too personal.
You smell so sharp and sweet
like lychee nuts and pineapple
and it fills me every time
a breeze crosses your skin.

Before this summer,
you always went for cucumber melon.

One sleepover two summers ago,
before Lars, I asked if I could borrow
a spray for my hoodie. I spritzed it
and thought of you
every time I put it on.

How could I not know
I had a crush on you then?

I am so lucky to know you.
Some people fantasize about kissing
but I remember holding your hand
when we were small.

When we were little,
I was always scared to go
to big birthday parties
or school carnivals.

You would take me by the hand
and say, "I won't have fun
without you."

I wish we could do the same now.

Your hand around mine—
leading me
into
the future.

JULY NIGHT

Chris,
    Sophia,
        and I walk home together.

There are fireflies out,
    even more than there were
        earlier in the summer.

Chris asks me
    if he can tell Sophia
        about "our plan" with our parents.

I tell him, "Haha—of course!"
    I know it means a lot to him.
        He's not "out" a lot of places

besides his Finsta
    and his Twitter,
        where he feels safe.

Sophia gets excited.
    She says,
        "Omg I want to help!"

We tell her
    we still need to figure out
        what we're doing.

We start bouncing around ideas.
    They get more and more absurd.
        Chris says, "We need to write it on balloons!!!"

I laugh and imagine
    a balloon cloud
        of rainbow colors.

Sophia says,
    "We need fireworks!
        Lots of them!"

I stop walking.
    I remember weekends
        when Chris and I were little.

We'd sit in our parent's laps
    and watch the town fair's fireworks
        as they dazzled around the houses.

The fair is on
    the last weekend of July.
        It seems like the perfect time.

I say, "What about at the fair?"
    They love the idea.
        Chris asks, "What do you have in mind at the fair?"

And I sigh because I don't know.
    At least it's a start.
        But still, how do you tell someone

a secret
    that's not
        a secret?

DINNER AT MY HOUSE

When we get home,
Mom has dinner just about ready.
She invites Sophia to stay but Sophia says,
        "Sorry, I promised Theo
        I would go to his house for dinner."

"Didn't you say he's working?"
I ask.

        "Yeah, but he likes to see me
        when he gets home," she says.

I want to shake her and say,
"He doesn't deserve you!"
and
"He's being controlling
and that's weird!"

But I don't—it doesn't seem right
with my family here

so I just say,
"Okay, have a nice time."

I hope she can hear
the hesitation in my voice.

I want to hug her goodbye but instead,
I just wave. I think the worst part
about coming out to her
is I like police everything I do, to make sure
I don't make her uncomfortable—

so that I don't seem like
I'm hitting on her or something.

Right now, I really just want
to feel close to my friend.

ME: Hey Soph, just wanted to say if you ever want to talk about stuff I'm here

ME: I know "stuff" is vague I just mean I know you've been dealing with a lot

Is that too vague not mentioning Theo?

I don't want her to know
I think he's a jerk

but I want her to know
I'll always listen to her.

She texts me right back.

SOPHIA: Thank you 😣

SOPHIA: Can you not text me till tomorrow?

That worries me
even more.

ME: Okay!

ME: I'm here if you need me!

LASAGNA

Mom tries a new recipe for lasagna
and I hate lasagna for that crumbly white cheese
but I would never complain about dinner to Mom.

She works so much and then makes us all food.
I've never made anything beyond like
boxed mac and cheese
and on the rare occasions Dad "makes" dinner
he always just orders pizza.

As usual, Dad is already sitting at the table
waiting for food.
Like why doesn't he help?

Anyway . . .
    He asks, "How was the show?"

I've told them
I have been "helping"
a person at the nursing home
but I haven't really said much
about Lena. I guess I'm worried
they'd think it's weird
to be friends with an older person
or they'd figure out
she's gay.

I say, "The show was great!"

DESCRIBING LENA

When I first started
hanging out with Lena,
I told Mom and Dad,
"Lena is the sweetest person ever.
We talk after work most days. She reads
and paints and writes.
She's like so cool—haha I wish I was
as cool as her."

> Mom had asked,
> "Does anyone else visit her?"

I told her the truth which is,
"Not that I've seen.
She says her family
is mostly gone."

> Mom said, "That's so sad . . .
> we should all go visit her
> one day."

I almost got the courage
to tell mom Lena is gay.

I felt like it could have been
a chance to see
how she'd feel about queer people.

I didn't do it though.

I was too scared
of her reaction.

Plus, even though
Lena and Mom will probably never meet,
it still didn't feel right

to "out" her.

TESTING THE WATERS

After dinner
back in our room,

I tell Chris,
"We should talk about someone gay
in front of Mom and Dad
to like see what they say."

Chris says, "That's not the same
as *us* being gay."

"I know
but we could at least learn something."

He thinks for a second.
"Maybe you're right.
Who can we say is gay?"

"We need like a celebrity—
someone they would know."

"Ellen?"

"Haha no that's too obvious.
Even Mom and Dad know
Ellen is gay."

"I mean it's not obvious to everyone."

"I mean it would be weird if we were like—
did you hear Ellen is gay?
She's been out like
our whole lives???"

"Good point . . ."

"What about . . . what about . . ."

"That newscaster on CNN!
What's his name?"

"Anderson Cooper?"

"No, no that's another Ellen situation.
The other one."

"Don Lemon?"

"Yes!"

"He's gay?" I ask.

"I think so, right?
It's perfect.
Mom even watches that sometimes."

"So, are you just going to say it at dinner?"
I ask.

"I'll think about it . . .
I also think I have an idea
for the coming-out thing . . ."

CHRIS'S IDEA

He sits next to me on my bed
so he can whisper.
He says, "I've been watching
all these videos. I want something
not too over-the-top. Something cute
and personal. The fireworks at the fair
are the perfect time. So what if,
when we're there,
we have them find clues
at each little thing we always do at the fair.
Like, we always go to see
the pie competition
and we always go to see the wood-carving show
and we always get home fries and funnel cake
and we always go on the Ferris wheel before the fireworks.

At each of those stops, we could give them
a piece of the message."

I worry that it's too complicated.
I kind of wish I could just tell them
as we watch the fireworks
but Chris is so excited,
so I tell him I like the idea.

What's funniest about it though
is that I didn't remember that those things
are what we always do at the fair.
He's totally right,
but I never realized it was a pattern
or a routine.

MY IDEAL COMING-OUT STORY

Would have nothing to do
with Mom and Dad
and it's a fantasy.

It would be me telling Sophia
"I'm bisexual,"

and her saying, "Me too!"

"And I've always loved you!"

Too bad
that opportunity
has passed . . .

The conversation
certainly didn't go
like that.

TIME IN THE SUMMER

Time moves differently in the summer.
Some days feel like weeks and some weeks feel like less than a
day.
I get into a routine at the nursing home and I actually kind of
love work.

At home, work gives me something to talk about with my
parents.
It's easy to talk about, only I keep not telling them Lena is gay.
I know it's not important but it feels like they can't understand

why I'm so friendly with her
because I don't feel like I can tell them.
Every day I tell myself I'll text Pen

and plan our next date
but days turn into more days and eventually,
a week passes without me saying anything.

It's not like I'm doing it on purpose.
I just feel like I can't think of what to say to her
and I'm scared to hang out again

because I feel like she's mad at me.
I know that's not true
and kinda not fair to her. She could also

text me first, though.
I wish that relationships
didn't sometimes feel like a job?

DRAMA PART 1

Most people who say they don't like drama
really do like it,
a little bit.

I'm not proud of it,
but I always want to know
what everyone's up to.

I don't like "drama"
but I also kind of do.

So, I'm excited
when Sophia calls me to talk.

I think
she's finally going to tell me about
what's happening
with Theo.

IT'S NOT ABOUT THEO

I go crazy whenever someone doesn't get right to the point
and they kind of talk around something

before they tell you
what you want to know.

We chitchat a little
about the show at the nursing home.

Then she pauses and says,
        "Pen texted me."

"She texted you?"

        "Yeah."

"What did she say??"

I want her to just come out and say it already.

"Last night after the show we went to,
    she asked if me and you were dating???"

"What?
Why would she do that?"

"I don't know, YOU tell me."

I don't understand.
Sophia sounds angry at me?

I haven't done anything to her.
Have I? I feel so guilty and gross.

Does she think I'm telling people that?

"I don't know, Sophia,
I would never tell people that."

Tears are welling up in my eyes.

"Because we're just friends.
    I wanted to tell you that."
    She pauses—
    her voice sounding
    balled up
    in her throat.

"You know that right?"

"Really, Sophia,
I never thought
otherwise."

I'm trying
not to cry
while I'm on the phone
with her.

"I'm sorry
I made you feel
like that."

She paused. "It's okay.
It just shook me up."

She adds,
"I've never talked to Pen much before
I thought you two were dating."

WHY WOULD PEN ASK IF ME AND SOPHIA WERE TOGETHER?

Did she see us together?
I thought she didn't want to be dating?

I keep apologizing to Sophia,
even though I feel like

I don't have anything
to apologize for.

She tells me it's okay and that she's sorry too,
for believing Pen. She tells me

we still need to hang out
and talk more soon.

Talk more
about what?

My brain
is an anxiety vortex.

I ask if we can just talk now
and she says,

"I have to think a little bit
about everything.

This is a lot

at once."

We hang up.

QUEER GIRL STEREOTYPES

I think the biggest queer girl stereotype
is that we're weirdly obsessed
with the girls we have crushes on.

The stereotype says
we can't help but fall in love
with our best friends.

There are all kinds of movies and shows
with crazy lesbians
pining for the straight friend.

In these shows, the lesbian
always starts stalking
or being creepy to the straight girl.

I hate how this makes queer girls
seem evil or bad
just for having feelings and emotions.

I feel so terrible for liking Sophia but
I keep thinking about her. I ask myself
if I really am doing something wrong

and I don't think I am.
I treat her like anyone
would treat their friend.

I just care about her.
She would be my best friend
no matter if she likes me romantically or not.

I hate that Pen has used our own stereotype against me.
Why do queer girls
hurt queer girls?

Still, now, something feels broken
between me and Sophia.
I know she didn't know all of this

but I can't help but feel like
she has been seeing me differently
since I came out to her.

ODE TO SUNDAY MORNINGS

Since I can't tell my family
I "go to different mass times" anymore

without you, Lars,
I'm stuck going to church.

I get up early, before everyone else.
I appreciate the birds chatting outside my window.

I look over and see Chris,
covers still pulled over his head.

Quietly, I sneak out to sit in the kitchen alone.
The living room and kitchen are almost the same room.

I usually hate our apartment's smallness
but this morning, by myself, I can appreciate it.

I note the pictures of Chris and me when we were little.
They sit on the bookshelf by cookbooks and magazines.

I think to myself,
this is my church,

alone with these small moments.
I wish I could explain this to Mom and Dad—

that going to church
has never felt like it's for me.

And it's not just because the Catholic church
doesn't support queer people like me.

It's also because I just hate sitting practically still
for hours and hours

listening to boring music
that makes me want to fall asleep.
I'm glad this is meaningful to some people
but it's just not right for me.

Maybe, Lars, you were kind of
my church when I still had you.

CHURCH BATHROOM

The church bathroom is a haven.

I go at least twice during mass

to just sit by myself.

In the bathroom, they play mass on speakers,

so I hear the singing. It echoes off the walls.

I scroll on my phone.

I haven't texted Sophia or Pen again.

I feel really sad and lonely—

like no one gets me.

    Like I'm drifting

           further away.

Ugh I'm so dramatic, aren't I?

I stand at the bathroom sinks. The room smells like bad flowery
perfume.

I look at myself in the mirror.

I look strange in my one nice "Sunday" dress.

My hair is wavy.

My eyes look tired.

I take as much time as possible

washing my hands. I think about

how the priest washes his hands before blessing the bread.

I think about miracles and I hope

there might be some

coming for me.

SISTER ANGELICA

Mass ends, and I walk out of the church with my family.
One of the parish nuns, Sister Angelica, greets us.

My family does church activities from time to time.
Mom helps with the women's group

and sometimes Dad does groundskeeping
to help keep the church garden looking nice.

Even Chris is an altar server. I'm the only one
who isn't really involved.

It's always kind of made me feel
separate from my family.

> "I haven't seen you in a while,
> so glad you're here,"
> Sister Angelica says to me.

I'm mortified. Are my parents going to find out
I've been skipping since I started driving myself?

"Oh really? I go every week,
just not to this mass,"
I say, shaking behind my smile.

Our church is pretty small,
so it's hard to miss someone.

I know I'm dead.
I don't dare look at my parents' faces.

> "Oh, I see," she says brightly.
> "Well, nice to see you all together."

I'm standing here thinking,
"How dare you rat me out, lady!"

I lie and say,
"It's great to be
together."

CAR RIDE HOME

Mom and Dad don't mention what Sister Angelica said. I realize
that not everyone thinks as much about every interaction—every
word—as I do. I think being queer makes you super aware of the
meaning of each word. I've spent so long trying to hide parts of
myself from some people while trying to share them with others.

COUNTDOWN: 350 DAYS

Sometimes when I feel really restless,
I start to count down the days until I can move out.
(Basically, until graduation.)

I know that some people stay with their parents after high school,
but I feel like I have to move out. Right. Away.

I don't even care what I do. Maybe I could just keep working
at the nursing home.

All day I feel like I can't focus or work on anything.
I mess around on my phone scrolling through Twitter.

I see Pen and Sophia have both retweeted things
and I don't know why,

but just seeing them online makes me angry.
More than anything,

I hate feeling angry.
I always don't know what to do
with anger.

ANOTHER COUNTDOWN: 20 DAYS

It's only twenty days
until we're supposed to come out
to our parents.

I don't know if I'll ever feel ready
or if I'll even end up
going through with it.

NURSING-HOME FOOD

When I work a full shift at the nursing home,
I'll eat a meal with the residents.

Lena almost never wants to come with me.
She says they aren't kind to her.

I've never seen anyone say anything
but I imagine they wouldn't in front of me since I work here.

I wish I could take her out of this place.
I wish I could give her somewhere to stay

where no one cared that she was gay.
At first, I didn't like the food, and I still hate the green beans,

but I'm really starting to get addicted to canned peaches
and tasty cakes. I always take an extra-tasty cake for Lena.

We sit on the end of her bed
before my break is over.

Today, I'm going to tell her
my plan to come out to my parents

and ask her
what she thinks.

CANNED PEACHES

We eat canned peaches from Styrofoam bowls.
Lena eats super slow and I always try to match her pace.

She tells me she likes to savor the sweetness.
Since this is the first time I'm seeing her since the show,

I tell her how awesome it was and how more people my age
should come.
She smiles and agrees. She's quieter than usual today.

I want to ask her why but I don't know how.
I ask her if she can help me with something.

　　　"Of course," she says.

"I want to come out to my parents.
My brother and I have a plan we think could work."

Her face looks very worried.
"What?" I ask.

　　"That can be hard. I'm sorry."
　　She says it like someone has died.

"I know," I say.
I pause, wondering if it's okay to ask this.
I decide to go for it
and see what she says.

"How did it go for you?" I ask.

　　"Oh, Claire.
　　I don't want you to think about that."
　　She furrows her brow
　　and shakes her head.

"Why?" I ask
and I regret it right away.
I shouldn't push her
if she doesn't want
to talk about it.

　　"It's not the same,"
　　she says firmly.

I'm quiet.
I understand.
I knew they didn't accept her
but I hoped at least
she would encourage me.

　　"Look, I want you to be happy.
　　It's hard for me to be encouraging though.
　　You never know what someone else will do or say.
　　I think it's most important to honor yourself.

That's really all we can do," she says,
scraping the syrup
from the bottom of her bowl of peaches.

The last part does make sense.
I just don't want to think of Mom and Dad
not accepting us.

The more I think about it—
the more I feel sure they won't.

I need to joke to lighten the mood.
"Will you adopt me if they don't accept me?"

Lena sighs.
"Don't say that . . .

but of course."

Lena squeezes my hand.

DATING IN YOUR EIGHTIES

Lena tells me,
"I have a date . . .
a real date with a woman next week."

She sounds concerned
and I'm like,
"Why don't you sound excited?"

Lena says,
"I don't know how to tell her
I live at a nursing home."
She gestures around.
"Not exactly glamorous.
Oh, if only I could have
shown her my house."

The other woman is the same age exactly
but she lives on her own.

> Lena says,
> "It makes me wonder
> why I can't be on my own like that.
> It feels unfair, but I know
> it's better I have the support here.
>
> When I moved out it was because
> I fell and hit my head.
> I waited for almost a whole day
> calling for help,
> until a delivery driver heard me.
>
> I was never so scared.
>
> I didn't want to die like that."

I don't know
what to tell her.

I never thought
anyone would be ashamed
of living there—

but then again,
I guess before working here,
I didn't really think

about what any of the residents
would want.

"That sounds scary,"
I say.

"I'm sorry."

> She waves her hand.
> "No use dwelling," she says

even though
she still sounds upset.

I change the subject
and I make a joke
about how Lena probably gets around
more than me.

Lena laughs before she says,
"Sometimes I wish
I didn't have to live here
or that I had
someone to stay with."

I tell her,
"I'm sorry. That sounds awful.
I wish it were easier."

I add,
"Maybe someday
we can live together
and I can look out for you."

"You have your own life to live,"
she says.

"My life can include yours, though,"
I say.

We hug and she tells me she'll always support me.
We cry.

I come back after my shift ends.

I put off going home later and later

and then visiting hours are over

and I have to leave.

LONG TEXT MESSAGES

I'll just say I hate them.

They always make me anxious
because I think of how long they took to write.

You can only write that much when:
1. You're in love.
2. You're super mad.
3. You're defending yourself.

On the walk home, I read
a long text message from Pen

and it's kind of all three.

PEN: I'm sorry I was such an idiot.
I love you Claire. I was just jealous of Sophia and I feel like you
like her. Like be honest you do like her don't you? I know you're
just friends. It was fucked up of me to tell her but
she has to know too, right? Just because I don't want to date
right now doesn't mean I don't want you to be honest with me. I
do love you but I'm not ready for a girlfriend.
I like you. Why is everything so hard? We should talk I know
but it's so hard to say what I mean in person. Maybe this week
we can get together. You don't have to respond just let me know
you got this. I've never liked a girl as much as I like you and
sometimes I don't know if it's you or just the summer and how
I'm just starting to learn about myself.

"ON READ"

I wish our phones didn't have the "read" or "unread" feature.
I opened Pen's message right away so I feel like I need to
respond,
but I have no idea what to say.

This summer feels like the first time I really
have no idea what to say to everyone:

Mom, Dad, Chris, Pen, Sophia—even Lena sometimes.

I feel like everything that's happening
doesn't fit into words.

Maybe that's why Lena writes poetry.
I think maybe I should write everyone poems.

What would it be like to actually talk in poems?

Every single word on every line would be
so deliberate and measured.

Haha I don't know if I could do it.

PEN'S POEM
THE PERKIOMEN TRAIL

When I think of you, I think of the gravel trail
and the lush green plants around it.
I think of the creek spilling cool water over rocks.
I think of us in the back seat of your car.

I crashed my car right before I met you.
It seems like a small thing
but it felt like losing a part of myself.

You filled me in again like the water fills in
the space between rocks.

What did I do wrong?

I HATE MY POEM

I hate my poem.

I want to delete it but I just save it.
I'll go back to it later.

For now, I actually text Pen back.

ME: Hey, thanks for telling me all that

ME: It is like brave to say all those things

ME: Can we take a walk on the trail tomorrow?

I hate talking in person
but I feel like I have to.

SCRIPTS

Sometimes I write scripts for myself
when I have to say difficult things.
The first time I did this was when
I got my first period.

For two days, I hoped it would go away. I threw away
four pairs of underwear. Each time, the stains were worse.
Finally, I wrote down what I wanted to tell my mom.
Of course, I knew what it was.

I just didn't want it to be real.
I kept a notecard with me when I asked to talk to Mom.
She seemed almost offended that I was so nervous about it.
I had wished I could just write her a letter to tell her.

I've been writing lots of scripts lately—sometimes just in my
head.
I play out the coming-out conversation between Mom, Dad,
Chris, and me.
I rehearse the conversations I wish I could have with Sophia
and tonight, I try to write out what I want to say to Pen.

BOY / GIRL PROBLEMS

Before I go to bed,
    Chris comes over
    and asks, "Hey, can we talk?"

I tell him, "Of course we can talk!"

    He pulls up his plastic desk chair.
    He says, "I like a boy
    and we're talking.

    It's been going on
    like all summer.

    I was going to die
    if I went another day

    without telling anyone."

"What! That's awesome!"
I say too loudly.

    "Shhh!" Chris says.
    "We're just talking.
    He likes me too though."

"Chris, that's great!"

    "But he's scared to be out or that
    we'll get caught."

"Are you not scared of that?"
I ask, curious about Chris.

    "I don't think I am anymore."

I don't feel the same way,
so I try to listen to Chris
as he talks about

just wanting to be free of this—
wishing it didn't have to be
a secret.

"It takes time.
Maybe the boy needs time.
We're still really young, you know?"

"I know.
It just sucks.
I've seen girls dating boys
since like fourth grade.
Why is it only 'too young'
for us to be ourselves?"

I hug Chris.
"I know, dude,
it sucks. It really does."

I don't plan to tell him
but I add,
"I think I want to come out to Mom and Dad
on my own.
Not together."

Chris looks hurt at first but he nods.
"I understand."

"I want to write them a poem,
I think.
Mom and Dad."

He nods.
"I don't know
what I should do."

"I'll still be beside you,"
I say.

"If you decide
to make it something big."

ODE TO RUNNING AWAY

Oh, Lars,
when was the first time
you dreamed of running away
from your life?

I pictured sliding
the key into your ignition
and speeding far away—

I would drive to the other coast—
maybe even to the Midwest.
Somewhere no one would find me.

Lush trees all around. A cabin
by a lake. A shack in the desert.
A tent among evergreens. An apartment
in a new city.

I would make
a fresh, bright home.

I would be a new person.
I'd be a waitress
or maybe open a flower shop.

I still think of escaping even without a car.
I close my eyes and see the bus routes
as they make veins across the state.

I know I'm being
dramatic. I just want
senior year to be over.

I want to
move away. I want to

be my own person.

I want to tell Mom and Dad
I'm queer
without feeling
so afraid.

THE TRUTH

Pen and I meet to talk.   I was nervous all morning.

I thought we might fight—   that we might yell at each other.

I wasn't sure what to expect.   I didn't get to know her that
long

and I've never really dated   someone where things felt so
electric.

We actually hug when I see her.   Her hair has new amethyst
highlights

and she is just as beautiful as ever.   I tell her, "I'm sorry,"

and she tells me, "I'm sorry too."   She says, "I was jealous
and kind of a bitch."

I say, "I was too." We laugh.   She says, "I kind of felt
like a placeholder."

"How so?" I ask.   She says, "Like I was second to Sophia."

I tell her I didn't want to admit it.   Pen takes my hand.

She says, "I had a good time though.

I thought I'd have to wait till I was older

to find a girl like me."

I tell her, "It doesn't have

to be totally over."

She says, "Uhhh it would kind of suck—

to keep dating

knowing you like someone else."

We walk the rest of the trail.   She asks, "Can we like kiss one
more time?"

We   kiss (?)

and I feel thankful for Pen.   She says she hates when people
ask,

"Can we still be friends?"   but she still wants to ask,

"Can we still be friends?"   I say, "Of course."

I GOOGLE "WHAT TO DO WHEN YOU LOVE YOUR BEST FRIEND? (GAY)"

And read article after article—
watch YouTube story times and vlogs
and scroll through a few blog posts.

Do we really fall in love
with straight people this often?

I guess you could just as easily say,
why do straight people
fall for gay people?
(Because that probably happens too.)

It's so hard because I don't want
to ruin our friendship.
Even that sounds cliché.
I wish it were easy
to tell each other the truth.

I don't know what's harder—
trying to tell Sophia I love her
or thinking of a way
to come out to my parents.

I alternate between stressing over both
all afternoon.

I kind of wonder
what would happen
if I didn't do either—

tell Sophia or come out—
would I just like
disappear? Explode
in a puff of smoke?

At this point,
I feel like I'm in too deep.

Not telling either of them
feels like completely disappearing.

SOPHIA: Hey did you still want to hang out?

ME: Yes!

It's late
but I want to anyway.

I tell Mom and
I step outside.

The cool air of the July night
blows against my neck.

I feel powerful
with my short hair.
I walk out toward her house.

I feel like I might
tell her
tonight.

SOPHIA IN PORCH-LIGHT GLOW

She gleams
like a bowl
of honey.

The bright ambers of her eyes.
Her melon-sweet smile.

She sits in a plastic lawn chair waiting for me.
Doesn't notice me at first,

just scrolling on her phone.
She leans back
before she sees me.

She stands up and says,
        "You're here!!!"

LEMONADE STAND

Seeing her on the porch
reminds me of one time
when we were kids—fifth grade,
so we thought
we were like super grown-up.

We made a lemonade stand
on her porch. Her house
doesn't have a lot of people walking by,
so she made a huge sign

that said WHEN LIFE GIVES YOU LEMONS
and waved it around.

Dozens and dozens of people came.
It was just crappy, powder-mix lemonade
but, like with everything, Sophia made it
a whole experience.

I just sat and mixed the drinks—
refilling the pitchers with ice
and making sure they were fresh.
It reminds me just how long

I've been in awe of Sophia.
Her infectious radiance.
How lucky I am to be
her friend.

COOL GRASS

We sit out in her yard like we always do.
We talk again about the talent show at the nursing home.
        Sophia tells me, "I'm trying to write poetry now.
                I know—I know, don't laugh.
                I just felt like inspired
                after hearing Lena's."

I tell her, "I have been trying too!
I'm not any good."

                She claps her hands together
                and says, "Here's a plan!
                Next sleepover we have,
                we should write poems together."

"I would love that,"
I say. "But you have to promise
that they're allowed to be
a little cringe."

"I in fact require
they be at least slightly
cringe," she says, laughing.

Sophia pauses.

A car drives past her house
and the summer bugs make music
of the night.

Sophia says, "I'm sorry for everything with Pen."
I wish I didn't say what I said."

"It's okay.
I understand,"
I say,
and I do

but it still hurts
that she was that afraid
of someone thinking
we were together.

Sophia says, "If I could do it over,
I wouldn't say anything
and I would trust you."

I appreciate how much she's trying.

WHAT WE DON'T SAY

Even though we talk about what Pen said,
we still don't go as deep as I want to about it.

It's like we're both ignoring the fact
I clearly do like her. I wish I could lie

and tell her I have no feelings at all for her,
but I can't. What I did say is true though:

I'd never want to make her uncomfortable.
All that power I felt when I left the house is gone

from the depth of what it seems like we just can't say.
Maybe it wasn't meant to be.

Maybe I should never "make a move." Maybe
we really can just stick to being friends

and feel thankful for that.
I'll meet so many other girls in my life,

or at least, that's what
I have to tell myself.

WHAT WE DO SAY

We talk about Theo and Pen.

I say, "How stereotypical is it for me
to literally have wanted to settle down with
the first girl I ever had sex with?"

I add, "It's okay to laugh,"

      and she does.

      Sophia says, "I can't believe myself
      with Theo."

"What do you mean?"
I ask.

      She sighs and says,
      "I think I convinced myself
      that Theo was the only boy
      who'd ever like me. You know because,"
      and she gestures broadly
      to herself.

"What? Sophia,
literally everyone thinks
you're amazing,"
I say.

          "Sure, but most of them
          don't know I'm trans.
          If they knew, it would be
          like so complicated," she says.

"I didn't think of that I guess.
I just think you're awesome,"
I say.

          "Thanks," she says.

"I don't think you should have to
come out to people if you don't want to,"
I say.

          "I know but I'd want someone I date
          to like know the whole me,"
          she says.

"I get that. I'm sorry.
But like there will be
all kinds of guys,"
I say, and pause to add,
"And plenty of ones
who like won't like
demand you spend
every waking moment with them."

          "Ugh, I was insane, Claire.
          How did I act like that?" she asks.

"Do you want to know
what I think?"
I ask.

"Only if it's not harsh," she says.

"It's not harsh to you,"
I say.

        "Okay go for it," she says.

"I think Theo was
kind of like brainwashing you.
Like I don't know but like
he made you spend
so much time with him
and then like made you feel
like you should be grateful for it.
A partner shouldn't do that,"
I say.

        "I didn't think of it like that.
        But now I feel like that's totally
        exactly what happened,"
        she says.

        "You know when we were together
        I like imagined marrying him
        and spending our lives together.
        I thought 'I can definitely make this work.'
        Like what the fuck, Sophia,
        you're only seventeen?"

"Haha it's not the Dark Ages,
we don't need to get married off
right away," I joke.

We laugh   and Sophia asks,
        "So you think
        people will love me?"

I want to tell her
I'll love her forever
as her friend

but I'm scared she'll think I mean
something else.

Sure, I still have feelings for her,
but tonight I'm learning
I could love her
as my best friend too.

"Yes, people will love you.
So many people,"
I say.

"PEOPLE"

Should I read more into that?
She didn't say "guys" or "men."

She said "people."

Hmmm, that's suspiciously
bisexual.

Relax, Claire!

Not everyone thinks
about every single word
like you do!

THIS FEELS EASY AGAIN

After talking for hours,
all of the tension between us is gone.

We drift around different topics.
I tell her that I want to come out to my parents this summer.
I tell her about how I want to write them a poem.

Sophia jokes that she wishes I still had my car
so we could drive away into the night
and be away from everything.

I ask what she means and she says
she just feels ready to leave our little town.

I tell her I am too.
Soon it's much later than I thought

and I head home.
She hugs me before I leave

and she smells sweet.
I wish I could hold her longer.

I LAY IN BED

And go back   and forth

about telling   Sophia how I feel.

There are signs   she might feel

the same   but she might also

just be my friend.   It's like this push

and pull   will never end.

I can't get   myself to stop thinking

should I or   shouldn't I

should I or   shouldn't I

tell her   how I feel.

NO COFFEE

Dad left for work last night.

Driving trucks means
he's gone for a few nights
and then back.

He has to leave
super, super early.

When he first started,
he used to kiss

me and Chris
on our foreheads before he left

but we got annoyed
getting woken up
in the middle
of the night

so he stopped.
Sometimes I want to ask him

if he could do it again.

I think I'd still hate getting woken up

but I also feel like I hardly see him.

He drank the last of the coffee
this morning

and the kitchen smells like it.

I groan,
looking at the used grounds,
trying to see if maybe

there's a sip left in the pot.

There really isn't.

Dad fills his thermos to the brim.

Guess I'm going to work
caffeine-less today.

LENA'S GIRLFRIEND

I have work today and my shift goes super slow
because there's not much to do.

I do my rounds, checking on residents
and making small talk.

I like the relaxed feeling but I also start to get super bored.
Usually, I try to wait till I'm done

to talk to Lena. But today I sneak away from the rec room
to sit with her.

She's excited to see me.
        She says, "Sit down, sit down! I have a secret to tell."

She holds up her iPhone.
It's another picture
of Marie.

In the picture, Marie
is forming a heart with her hands.

The text message
below it reads,
"Lena you have stolen
my heart."

        Lena says, "We're making it official.
        We decided to be girlfriends last night.
        Can you believe that?"

        Lena laughs.
        "Girlfriends and I've never
        even met her in person."

"We have to change that!"
I say.

        "We sure do," she says.

FIRST DATE

"And here, kiddo,
is where I need your help," she says.

"Now, I know other residents have had dates
but none of them are lesbians.
I don't know how it would,
you know . . . go over.

I feel too afraid
to bring her here."

I don't think anyone would say anything
but I'm not sure.

I'm thinking about
how it's not fair she
has to feel afraid.

This is her home.
She deserves to feel safe.

"I promise I'll help however I can,"
I say.
"I just have to come up
with a plan."

Lena isn't allowed to leave the home
without an escort
because of her dementia.

That's a rule for everyone
on her floor.

We never talk about this directly—
it's kind of just like understood
between us.

When she explained
why she started living at the home,

she never mentions it either—
she just talks about
the time she fell.

Sometimes I wonder
if there's more to what happened
but I also know
that's her life and
she can choose what she wants
to share with me.

She seems like
she remembers as much as
anyone would but
she also has support systems here
that she wouldn't
on her own.

THIS IS KIND OF COMPLICATED

"Maybe we could pretend Marie is your sister
here to take you out to lunch!" I say.

Lena says, "They might check her license."

I say, "Maybe cousin?"

Lena wonders aloud,
"Would they let a random cousin come?
I've never had anyone visit before."

"Maybe you could just tell them
the truth?"
I ask and then I wonder
if it's right for me
to ask Lena that.

But, after all,
don't they already know she's queer from her poems
and her decorations?

Lena says, "I'm scared they would tell me
I don't know myself. Because you know—
you know because I have memory issues.
I'm scared they'd just say
me being gay is me being crazy."

Lena swallows.
She's close to tears.

And I feel terrible
for prying.

"I'm sorry—"
I start to say.

"No no—it's not you.
I just worked so hard
to live as myself—
why do I still have to be fighting?"

I'm like,
"How could anyone think that?!"

Lena tells me, "It's happened though, Claire.
I've seen it happen.
I've had friends who couldn't see their girlfriends
in nursing homes and hospices.
I've seen families
keep people's lifelong partners
apart from them.
It's terrible."

"I'm going to fight anyone
who would say that about you,"
I say.

Lena smiles.
"Oh, stop that.
We're going
to figure this out.

Don't lose your job
for me."

"I would though!
Watch me!"
I'm half joking
but also
mostly not.

I HAVE AN IDEA!

I ask,
"What if she's a volunteer?"
The home has all kinds of volunteers
who take residents out.
She'd just need to fill out a form
and go to the short training."

Lena sits thinking
and she's nodding along.

"Then, you would just need to request
to go to town with a volunteer!
Bingo! There we got it!"

Lena smiles
and says, "That might just work!"

WHEN MY SUPERVISOR WALKS IN

I'm sitting on the edge of Lena's bed,
helping her type out a message to Marie, her girlfriend,
but it looks like I'm just on my phone
in the middle of work.

My supervisor has always been really nice to me
but now she speaks sternly.

"Claire! We have been looking for you.
Mr. Summers needs his bedding changed
and two other residents need their afternoon snacks.
What are you doing here?
Lena isn't on your caseload today?"

I look at Lena and I know I can't explain everything.
I fumble for a few seconds, starting and stopping
before saying, "Lena asked me for help with her phone."
And it sounds like a stupid excuse
but it's something? Right?

I TAKE IT BACK I DON'T WANT TO GET FIRED

She tells me I need to come with her
and for the next fifteen minutes,
she talks to me in her office.

She tells me she's happy I connect with the residents
but it can't get in the way of my job.
I want to cry but hold it in.
I need to be professional.

I get back to work, trying my best to pay attention
to every little detail. I almost never get in trouble
at work or school and it feels so uncomfortable

but I also feel mad. I don't feel like
I was really doing anything wrong.

ODE TO COMPLAINING

It doesn't always help
but sometimes everyone needs to complain.

I get home from work and sprawl out on my bed.

Chris walks in and closes the door.
He lays down on his bed too.

"What's up?" he asks.

"Work was annoying," I say.

"Want to complain?"

"My boss just was upset
I was hanging out with Lena
instead of doing rounds."

"I bet you were helping her.
Isn't that also basically your job?"

"Exactly!"

I roll over and sit up.

"She literally has a girlfriend.
She's getting more action than us."

"Nice!
An icon."

"Only she's worried they won't let her girlfriend
take her out for a date."

"Why the hell not?"

"Because only certain people can take her out."

"That's dumb."

"Right?
But don't worry.
We have a plan."

I walk over to my bag
and get out the volunteer form.

"We're going to have her girlfriend sign up
to volunteer and then take her on a date."

"Ha! That's quite a plan."

"I hope it works.
Lena is so excited.

How's *your* plan coming?"

Chris sighs.

"I don't know.
I want to come out and I have the date set.
I guess I just don't know
what reaction I'd even want."

WHAT DO I WANT?

We talk about how
it's hard to know what we'd want our parents to say.

Do we want them
to be super excited and become LGBTQIA+ activists?

I'm not sure. Probably not.
Seems kind of exhausting.

Am I being too picky?

I guess maybe I just want them to see me
for who I am.

Sometimes, I think I'm not just worried
about coming out.

I want my parents to think
I'm perfect in so many ways.

I want them to see me
as a good Catholic person
and student
and worker
and girl
and daughter
and sister.

I feel like there's so many things
I want to "come out" to them about.

Maybe what was also so hard
about losing you, Lars,
was how it showed I'm not perfect

the way I want them to see me—
the way I wanted to think of myself.

OVER FAMILY DINNER

We're all quiet.

We're usually quieter
when Dad isn't home.

I miss when he's not here.

It's like no one knows
what to say
and at least Dad is good
at nudging along
some small talk.

Chris looks at me
as if to ask
what's wrong?

I look back to reply
that I don't know.

Dinner is mac and cheese,
which means
Mom didn't feel like cooking.

Which means
something is wrong.

I go through my brain
trying to think of

what I might have done wrong.

DAD WALKS IN

And I know
this isn't normal.

Dad travels with his cargo
for days.

Something must be wrong
if he's home early.

Did Mom know?

He must have texted her.

> "Hey," he says,
> looking haggard.

>> "You said you'd be here
>> before dinnertime,"
>> Mom says.

> "I tried—" he starts

>> and she puts up her hands.
>> "It's all right.
>> We just started."

> "All right.
> Well. No easy way to say this
> but, Chris, we have to talk a little.
> Man to man, right?"

Chris swallows
the lump of mac and cheese
that he just bit down on.

I knew something was weird
with Mom.

I don't know what's going on though.

Dad never talks to us.

My parents in general never ask
"to talk to us"

unless it's something
really
bad.

PART 4

Odes to This July

I WANT TO GO WITH THEM

But Dad and Chris leave

and I'm just sitting
with Mom

while she takes away the dishes
and places leftovers

in Tupperware.

THE AIR IS TENSE

I think
about
how much
I don't know
about
my mom.

I remember
when I
was little
we used to play
"cooking show"
and I would
pretend
to be the host
while she
made dinner.

I wonder
if it's
kind of
my fault
we aren't
close anymore.

I wonder
if we can
be close again.

What would
that look like
now that I'm older?

Can I still
learn to be myself
and be independent
and trusted

and also share
that self
with
my mom?

SO, I SAY IT

"Mom?"

     "Yes?"

"I miss
playing cooking-show host
with you.
Do you remember that?"

     "Of course, I remember.
     I thought you might have
     forgotten."

"I want to play that again,"
I say,
only half joking.

     She laughs.
     "All right.

What are we
going to make?"

I think for a second.
"Something fancy
like macarons."

Mom scoffs.
"We would make
disaster macarons."

"Might be fun to try sometime."

"Sometime," she says.
"That could be fun."

"ARE YOU MAD AT ME?"

Mom sighs.

"Honey, I'm not mad at you.
We're just worried."

I can't understand
what she would be worried about?

Chris and I both had good grades
at the end of school.

I even have a job
and I have Sophia
and Lena as friends.

What else could I be?

"About what?" I ask.

"You guys don't talk to us anymore.
You're . . . scared of us.
You avoid us and we have to wonder
what you don't want us to know."

"I'm not scared of you,"
I say, even though
I realize I am kind of scared of them.
Especially Mom
because she's home more.

 "That doesn't sound convincing,"
 Mom jokes.

"You don't understand,"
I say, looking down
at the kitchen table.

 "Not if you don't let me."

Something gives me the bravery to say,
"I feel like
you're always
judging me.
How could I
tell you
about my life?"

ODE TO MOM

Her voice is the color orange. Her feet are like smooth stones
in a creek. Her hands are steady the way
the horizon always seems smooth and even.

When we used to go
back-to-school-clothes shopping each August,
She would wait outside the dressing room
and bring me more and more jeans and tops

and skirts and shorts to try on—
telling me they all looked perfect on me.
She sweeps hair from the floor of the salon.

Trash cans full of hair. I wonder if she ever wants
to have a different job or a different life. I wonder if she wishes
we had a house again instead of this apartment.

She would do anything for us. She wears
lavender perfume. She is so beautiful.
I wonder if I'm anything like her.

IT IS HARD TO TRUST SOMEONE

I almost tell Mom
all of the truths.

I almost come out. Almost admit
to all the times I've lied
about where I'm going
because the truth was too complicated.

I'm so close but I still get scared.

Instead, I tell her part of the truth—
that Sophia and me have had
"some drama" in the past few weeks.

I say,
"She's my best friend you know
and she like ghosted me
for this guy."

> "I bet he was a pig.
> That Sophia is too nice for boys your age,"
> she says.

I disagree how she says it
but I just want to bond with my mom
so I say,
"I know right?
He sucked!
She's finally broken up with him now

but it kind of messed up
the start of my summer."

> "Do you want me
> to call his mom?" she asks.

I laugh.
"Mom what the heck
would that do?"

> She shrugs.
> "Let him know
> we mean business."

"No.
But thank you,"
I say.

ABOUT CHRIS

Mom asks if I know about Chris.

I'm not sure
if she knows
what I know.

I want to trust her with everything.
I just can't.
Not yet.
Soon.
Soon.
Soon.

WHAT MY PARENTS THINK

I feel like they always assume
the worst of us.
I hate that.
Dad wanted to talk to Chris because

he noticed Chris "sneaking around"
aka he noticed Chris
hasn't been home as much.
He's always walking around town
going to visit
the boy he likes.
Half the time I don't even know where he is.
I still don't even know
the guy's name
because Chris
won't tell me.
Dad thought he was on drugs.
Why is that where everyone's brain goes to?
Also like if he was using drugs
this probably wouldn't be the best way to help him.
It's sad but also kind of funny
that he would assume
anything other than the truth—
his kids are queer
and scared of him.
I love my dad but sometimes I feel like
he doesn't know
how to talk to us.
We used to go fishing
on weekends as kids.
We used to take long drives
to the flea markets
but not since he's had to work more.
It's hard to talk to him
unless you're doing something.
At least he didn't actually figure out
Chris is gay.
I was scared for him.
Maybe it wouldn't be bad
but still,

Chris should be able
to decide
when he wants
to come out.

CLOSE CALL

Back in our bedroom,
we text instead of talking
because we don't want
Mom and Dad to hear us
and after everything at dinner,
we think they're defs listening.

ME: That was . . . uhhh lot

CHRIS: You're telling me!

CHRIS: I thought I was literally going to get kicked out

ME: I'm sorry 😞

ME: Do you want a hug?

CHRIS: No

CHRIS: Yes

I get up and hug him
and then go back
to my bed.

ME: In that kind of situation like if they were mad at you for being gay . . . what would you want me to do?

CHRIS: What even could you do?

CHRIS: Fight them haha

ME: I would!

ME: Don't tempt me

CHRIS: I guess just back me up

CHRIS: Tell them I'm still their son

CHRIS: Tell them being gay isn't a huge deal

CHRIS: Really, I almost wish you could come out for me.

CHRIS: Like you could be like "hey mom and dad in case you didn't notice, Chris is gay. I'll field any questions.

ME: Haha I mean I would

CHRIS: I don't know.

CHRIS: I should probably do it

ME: Let me know!

ME: I love you!

CHRIS: ily too

OPERATION: LENA'S DATE

The next day after work,
I stop over at Sophia's house
and I tell her about Lena's date.

We share a bowl of blueberries
on her sofa.

Me and Lena just helped Marie submit
her volunteer application
and we're hoping it'll get accepted
by tomorrow.

We also exchanged cell numbers
and I don't know why we hadn't before.

I saw her use her cell phone
but because she's old I was just like,
"Oh she probably can't text."

I've heard the term "ageist" before
but I didn't think about it much.
I think I was kind of being ageist though
without realizing it—just assuming
she didn't know anything
about texting
because she's old.

Sophia says,
"What can I do to help?
This is like the most exciting thing
that's happened all summer."

I want to ask her
if it's more exciting
than her time with Theo
but I have to let it go.

She's moving on so,
so should I.

"I'll think about it.
I'm sure we could use
your expertise somewhere,"
I say.

"This is amazing.
How old is Lena again?"

"Eighty-five,"
I say.

"Damn.
Lesbian royalty," she says.
"Is she from here?"

"Yes but
she used to live in Philly,"
I say.

She nods.
"Makes sense.
More queer people there.
That's where I have to go
to see my hormone doctor.
Do you think I could like
visit Lena sometime?"

"I think she'd love that,"
I say.
"You totally should."

Then, I have this crazy thought
of asking Sophia if we can go
on a double date
with Lena and Marie

but that would be in a world
where Sophia
was into me like that.

OPERATION: CHRIS COMING OUT

Is not going quite as well
as operation: Lena's date.

After Dad had that "talk" with Chris,

he doesn't want to come out at all.

He tells me tonight, "I just don't feel like
I can handle it if they don't accept me.
It doesn't seem worth it."

I understand what he means.

I tell him,
"You don't have to stick to the date you set.
at the end of the month."

Chris says, "If I let that date pass,
I'm worried I'll never tell them."

ME: Has Marie gotten her application accepted?

LENA: yeppers!

ME: Omg!

ME: Is there anything else she needs to do?

ME: Isn't there like training?

LENA: It's not a long training

LENA: She's actually coming in today to do it!

LENA: They told her they can do training and then she's free to participate in the volunteer day

LENA: I'm so nervous

LENA: I hope she likes me in person

ME: It'll be okay

ME: How could she not Lena you're a catch!

ME: I'm going to come over to help

LENA: aren't you off?

ME: I don't care!

ODE TO MARIE'S CAR

Blue Thunderbird, glinting in the sun.
It pulls up to the nursing home. I'm off today,
so I come over just to help make sure
Marie and Lena get paired together.

On volunteer days, a handful of different volunteers come
and they're usually paired randomly with residents.

I'm going to try to rig the system, though,
and write down Lena's and Marie's names on the volunteer
sheet.

This is risky because
I'm kind of tampering with the home's documents
but really does it matter if I'm helping Lena out?
She is a resident, after all.

Sophia comes with me to make me look
less suspicious. Our alibi is that I'm bringing Sophia here
to get her own volunteer application,
which is true. I'm actually doing that too.

Sophia is excited.
I haven't seen her this into something
since we came up with the plan to hook up
in our crushes' cars this summer.
(Hopefully, this turns out better.)

Sophia tugs my arm and points at Marie's car.

> "Oh my gosh!
> That's her! Isn't it?" she says.

Marie has huge sunglasses
and a colorful silk bonnet.

Her lipstick is bright blue
and her nails are painted bright red.
I hope I have this much style
when I'm eighty.

MEETING MARIE

She recognizes us right away
as she steps out of her car.

> She embraces us and
> says, "You're just like Lena said!"

Marie smells like rose petals.
She says with a wink,
"I'm so happy there are
young people just like us
willing to break some rules."

Sophia doesn't notice
but I do. When Marie says "people just like us,"
I think she means lesbians! She thinks
Sophia and I are together!

Does that mean Lena TOLD her we're together????
I'm going to be so annoyed if she did.

I know she wants to encourage me
but that's not helpful at all.

Does she not understand
Sophia isn't sure about her sexuality?

Forcing someone into something
isn't going to help anyone discover themselves.

And I just have to accept that.

I mean Sophia might not ever know
and that would be okay too.

ACCORDING TO PLAN

So much of this summer has felt like a complete mess;
it's so exciting when everything goes right with Lena and Marie.

Sophia distracts the coordinator by asking her questions
while I edit the volunteer list to pair them together.

No one notices! They go out to brunch together
and we come along because they say they want to "treat us"

for all our help. It doesn't feel like I did much
but they are so grateful. Marie says she's going to come

every Tuesday to "volunteer." We laugh.
They tell us about what it was like when they were girls.

Marie didn't know she was gay till she was thirty!
        She says, "I just never had the language for it."

I feel lucky in that way—that these people came before me
and made space for other queer girls.

Sophia seems like she's having a really nice time too.
Before Marie drives us back,

        Sophia says, "I want to do this every week!
        But I'm sure you guys will want dates without us."

I say, "Maybe every once in a while.
I want to go out together again."

We all agree and happily finish our piles of pancakes
and waffles, coffee, and orange juice.

QUEER GRANDMOM

I want to be a queer grandmom one day.
I'll bake rainbow-flag cookies
and let queer kids hang out in my house all the time.

I know it doesn't make sense
but before Lena I had never even really considered
that there might be queer people much older than me.

Maybe in their twenties, but not their forties and fifties and
so on.
I wish there was a place to meet queer people
of all ages. I want to know about their lives and tell them about
mine.

SOPHIA AND ME

After Marie and Lena leave,
we talk about the summer after elementary school
and how grown-up we thought we were.
We bought wallets at the dollar store
to house our quarters. We spent afternoons
at the pool applying sunscreen to each other's shoulders.
We had been so scared to go to middle school
and now look at us! About to start senior year.

I start to wonder to myself
what it would be like to have a girlfriend in school.
Would our friends be accepting?
I would hope they would be but it doesn't matter
because Pen and I broke up (if you can call that breaking up).

Sophia asks if I want to come over tomorrow.
I tell her I have work but the day after I could.
She hugs me before I go and tells me again
how fun she thought today was.
I try to keep the hug brief.
I remind myself:
We're just friends.
We're just friends.
We're just friends.
We're just friends.
We're just friends.
We're just friends.
We're just friends.
We're just friends.
We're just friends.
We're just friends.
We're just friends.
We're just friends.
We're just friends.
We're just friends.

We're just friends.
We're just friends.
We're just friends.

COUNTDOWN: 10 DAYS

Something about spending time with Lena and Marie
makes me feel like I do actually want to come out.

I'm not sure if it's safe but I don't know
how I could go on without coming out to my family.

Everyone. I want to tell everyone!
It's not even because I'm scared anymore.

I feel connected to other people more
than ever before. Hundreds of years of queer women behind me.

"I want to do it," I say to Chris.
We had been sitting quietly in our room.

    "What?"

"Come out. I think you were right.
I want to come out at the fair."

    "Me too."

ESCAPE PLANS

Chris and I brainstorm what to do
if our parents don't accept us.

Chris will stay with his friend Ian up the street
and I will stay with Sophia.

I hate to think like this
but having a plan makes coming out feel

more possible. When I asked Sophia over text,
she told me, "Of course you can stay with me

but don't worry so much—your parents are cool.
I'm sure they won't care Chris and you are gay."

That made me so angry.
How would she know

what it's like?
I've heard so many stories

of people being kicked out for being queer.
You don't know how someone will react—

good or bad.

POEM FOR MY PARENTS

I want you to love me for who I am

    even though I'm not sure I know who you are.

Dad, I miss our long drives.

    I miss when you'd pick me up

        and put me on your shoulders.

Mom, I miss cooking with you.

    I miss watching *American Idol* with you

        and sitting in the cart while you shopped for groceries.

Is it my fault we all feel distant?

    Is it my fault we don't have as many things as we used to?

        Is it my fault our family feels distant from each other?

No matter what happens,

    I think I'll love you

        always.

U-HAULING IT

After another shift, I sit with Lena
and she jokes that Marie and her are too old to "U-Haul it."

I laugh and ask, "Do lesbians really do that?"

Lena thinks for a minute, then says, "I sure have.
The thing about queer stereotypes
is that they never quite capture
the whole picture."

"What do you mean?"
I ask.

"Well, I think queer women want to move in with each other
so fast because it can be so hard and feel so rare
to find each other and really connect."

I have never thought of the stereotype
that lesbians fall in love too fast
like that. It makes so much sense.

I imagine Sophia and me piling all our things
into a shared U-Haul truck.
I lift her favorite wall tapestry
and she carries my orange-tasseled lamp.

"Sadly, I think Marie and I will have to just
enjoy our dates.
I was so happy you could come that first time.
What are you doing about Sophia?"

This makes me upset.
I told her Sophia is probably straight.
Why does she have to keep pressing?

"She's good. We're good."
I say.

"Are you really, dear?"

I don't want to cry,
so I swallow it.

It's so hard feeling so close to someone
and knowing you can't ever be with them.

　　"I think you should tell her."

"That won't make her not straight,"
I say softly.

　　"No, but regardless of how she feels
　　it can help both of you grow."

"Or fall apart."
I say.

　　"I know it's hard sweetie, I know,"
　　she says.

STRAIGHT

Back at home
after talking to Lena,
I'm kind of thinking
maybe it's not fair
that I keep saying
Sophia is probably straight
just because
she's not sure
about her sexuality.
Why should we default
to thinking everyone is straight?
I guess I started saying that
to try to protect myself—
to not feel so bad
if she doesn't like me back.
The truth is, though,
she could be lesbian or bi

or pan or queer
and also, not like me back.

CHRIS'S CRUSH

Whenever Chris tells me about the boy he likes,
he makes me swear a million times that I
won't tell anyone—that I remember it's
just a crush—that they aren't dating,
just talking. The boy seems to like
him back though. I want to tell
Chris to go for it—to tell this
boy he doesn't just want to
flirt. I know that's hard.
When we talk tonight,
I can see how all of
this is hollowing
Chris out. He
feels like he
can't be
fully him-
self any-
where.

ODE TO JULY

Dad used to say,
> "There's one perfect night in July
> where the most fireflies are out,

> > when the night is tinged cool and blue
> > and everything feels perfect in the world."

July feels like another planet this summer. Senior year is still
far enough away to ignore.
> So much has changed.

It scares me
how different I am
from who I was last year.

I wasn't even really out to myself last year.
Sophia and I were best friends.

We drew with sidewalk chalk
on her driveway
and ate sugary popsicles all day.

It takes too long to grow up.

Will I always remember this July?
This July, where I lost you, Lars?

Right now, it feels like everything is happening
at once but maybe years from now, maybe
I'll forget the details.

Maybe Mom and Dad will
accept us so easily,
I'll forget just how scared I was.
And I'll fall
out of love with Sophia
and laugh

about how crazy

I was for her.

COUNTDOWN: 5 DAYS

I admit to Chris, "I'm counting down the days
until we come out to Mom and Dad."

Dad is home and happy to be off from work,

so he cuts up a ripe watermelon.

The juice drips all over the counter.

We talk and eat all together. It's hard to live

in such a small space but I do love them all sometimes.

That night, we take another walk.

I say, "We need a plan,"

even though this summer

has been a summer of plans gone awry.

Maybe we don't need a plan?

Do we just say,

"Hey, Mom, Dad, we're queer!"?

Should we make a poster?

A PowerPoint?

Note cards?

A speech?

Write it in fireworks?

RUNNING INTO PEN

I take a walk to the creek alone.
I listen to sad music: Death Cab for Cutie and Sufjan Stevens.

What do I even have to feel sad about?
I sit down on a bench near the creek to watch

the ducks float by. I'm trying to clear my mind
but it ends up just making me feel even more cluttered.

What if what if what if what if what if what if . . .

I flinch and jump up as someone taps my shoulder.
I get into a fighting stance and then relax

when I see it's just Pen.

I flush. I'm embarrassed to see her especially at the creek

where we had sex. She smiles, which relaxes me a little.
She asks if she can sit with me and I say, "Of course!"

Pen asks, "How've you been?"

I say, "I've been better."

Pen says, "Me too. I kinda miss hanging out."

Now my brain is totally mixed up.
She misses me? Do I miss her?

I remind myself
you can miss people as friends

but I know there's always going to be
a little spark of something else
between us, at least for me.

"Not like romantically—not anymore.
Just like as friends," she adds.

"Oh I see.
What uhhhh
brings you here?"

"Clearing my head."

"Ha, me too.
It's not working."

"Trying to stop thinking
about Sophia?" Pen teases.

I flush even brighter.

She points at me. "I knew it.
Knew it knew it knew it."

"I know. I know.
You do know she's going
to stop being my friend

if I tell her though,
right?"

Pen shrugs. "I don't know,
you could be surprised."

"Or surprised in a bad way.
I'd like fewer bad surprises.
I feel like this kind of thing happens all the time—
queer people falling for their best friend
who isn't interested."

"I want to make it my personal mission
to make queer women talk to each other.
I mean, Claire, I could be wrong,
but I have gaydar and there's no way
Sophia doesn't at least have
some of the same feelings as you do.
I've seen you together;
you're like inseparable."

"We're just super-close friends,"
I say, and even I don't buy it.

Here I am repeating
the same nonsense straight historians say
about clearly lesbian couples.

"I guess I just feel like
we don't always tell each other how we feel
and I think Sophia is some non-straight sexuality."

I sit with that for a second.
"What makes you say that?
Other than like
us being close."

"It's just a vibe I get.
A 'bi-be,' you could say."

"Argh that's terrible

but I like the substitute for 'gaydar.'"

>"All I'm saying is,
>I think you should actually talk about it.
>Maybe she doesn't like you
>but I just think she does."

I smile. "Pen, you're like
a queer guardian angel."

>"Without the angel,"
>Pen says. "That's the Catholic in you talking."

"Yuck, oh God it is."

We laugh and toss stones
into the water.

COUNTDOWN: 3 DAYS

It's all I can think about.

Chris and I have lists
of our coming-out ideas all over the floor.

None of them are right.
He cries and I tell him that
whatever happens,

it will be okay.

We have dinner all together.

Dad will be home for a few days
and wants to spend time with us.

He asks how work is
and it's hard to tell him
without talking about Lena

and it's hard to talk about Lena
without talking about her girlfriend.
Telling partial truths only makes it

harder to feel connected.
He makes us a fruit salad
which is his form of cooking.

Juice drips down our chins
and I share a look with Chris.
It feels so melancholy

that we have to feel far away from
Mom and Dad. Sometimes I feel like
it's my fault—like I'm making a huge deal

out of nothing. But, alone with Chris
in our room, I feel like really fully me.
Soon Mom and Dad will see it too.

I just hope they like what they see.

SOPHIA AND ME / ME AND SOPHIA

The days feel fast and slow.
I finish a shift at the nursing home
and check my phone to find
a text from Sophia.

SOPHIA: Do you want to go
to the fair this Friday?

I freeze, standing on the sidewalk.
I want to tell her "no" because
I'm supposed to go with my family
but I always go with Sophia too.

ME: Maybe Saturday?

SOPHIA: Aw but I want to see the fireworks with you. Do you have work? ☹

I decide I should just tell her
the truth but it makes me feel
so vulnerable. Will she think
it's dumb to come out like this?

ME: No . . . I don't.

ME: Me and Chris just have this plan
to come out to our parents at the fair.

SOPHIA: Aw that's sweet.

SOPHIA: I want to like support you.

SOPHIA: Is there anything I can do?

ME: Haha, can you make my parents not be homophobic?

SOPHIA: ☺ Maybe. you never know.

SOPHIA: I'll work my transgirl magic.

I know she's trying to be nice
but that makes me feel sad.

What if it goes really badly
and Sophia is there to see it too?
Ugh, can't I just avoid this forever?

ME: Can I ask you something?

SOPHIA: Sure?

ME: How did your parents react?

ME: Like when you came out.

ME: You always told me it was good.

ME: But like was it hard a little bit too?

SOPHIA: Omg of course

SOPHIA: It was like some of the hardest days of my life

SOPHIA: They were supportive and all

SOPHIA: But they were emotional too and I felt like it was all my fault that they had emotions.

SOPHIA: I felt like I wanted to take it back to make things easier

ME: Oh no that's . . . that's so hard

SOPHIA: But like I'm glad I did

SOPHIA: It wasn't really like an option not to for me

SOPHIA: It's really different for everyone though

SOPHIA: Just know I'm here for you

SOPHIA: And I love you

I hold the phone.

I know it's a friendly "I love you,"

but it still makes me swoon a little.

ME: Well, at least if my parents kick me out we know your parents will let me crash there if I needed to

SOPHIA: Only if you're ready to accept a bi-pride-flag cake

ME: Always!

ME: Thanks for telling me that

ME: I actually feel less stressed now

ME: I know gender and sexuality are different but I feel like much less alone in my thought spirals

ME: I really am sorry if I ever made you feel
like uncomfortable like with the stuff Pen told you.

SOPHIA: Oh no—that was honestly my fault.
I'm sorry I reacted shitty. I just—
I just like never expected it and then
I was thinking about it and I got scared.

ME: Scared?

SOPHIA: Of our friendship getting fucked up
and like I never even really let myself think
about liking a girl—it just kind of
made me think about like identity and stuff.

ME: Oh totally.

ME: Hey you rock 😊

I want to tell her
        so much more.

SOPHIA: You too! Let's meet before the fair.
We can walk together.

ME: Perfect.

ME: My mom will be getting back from work
so they'll come together a little late anyway.

YEARS AFTER HIGH SCHOOL

I wonder

        what I remember of all this.

I wonder

        if Sophia will still be my best friend.

I wonder

        how I will feel about my parents.

I wonder

> how long my hair will be.

I wonder

> if I will visit Marie and Lena.

I wonder

> if I can become someone new.

I wonder

> if we ever really change.

I wonder

> who will be there to hold me.

COUNTDOWN: 2 DAYS

I'm so happy to have to work
to keep my mind off everything.

I ask Lena when I stop by after my shift,
"What were you like
in high school?"

I know it's kind of random
but I want to know.

> Lena laughs. "A troublemaker," she says.

I can't imagine Lena
being anything but as sweet and kind
as she is.

> Lena adds, "It was good trouble though.
> I protested my school board
> to let girls join the honors science classes
> because they used to only have those
> for boys."

"Omg Lena, feminist icon,"
I say.

> Lena rolls her eyes. "I wouldn't say that."
> She smiles. "I did have fun causing trouble though."

"You definitely
make me feel like I'm super boring,"
I say. "I'm sorry but
I have to topic-change
because it's like
all I can think about."

I tell her,
"I think I am really
going to tell Sophia I love her."

> Lena takes my hand
> and tells me, "Do what you think
> is best. I shouldn't have pushed you so much.
> Everyone's life is different."

Now I'm even more confused.
"Wait, so do you think
I shouldn't tell her?"

> Lena laughs. "No, no, I'm just saying
> it's only ever your choice to make."

That's comforting
but I also kind of wish she could
just tell me what to do.

"Did you ever tell a girl
you loved her
when you were
in high school?"

> Lena frowns. "No, but I wish I could have.
> My best friend meant so much to me.

We fell out of touch though.
I think I didn't have the words
to name why I felt so attached to her.
Maybe in a way,
we were practically dating.
She thought I was
sometimes too clingy with her.
I mean it's obvious now why.
I didn't know I was in love with her then
but I do now."

That makes me so sad
but I also feel lucky
to have words like
"bisexual" to describe myself.

Lena and I hug again
and she tells me,

> "I know you'll figure out
> what feels right."

ODE TO A CAR RIDE WITH DAD

After work,
Dad surprises me by picking me up.
He wasn't sure what time I'd be done,
so he just sat in the parking lot
reading the comics in his front seat.
Dad will literally buy the paper on Sundays
just to pull out the comics section
to read during the week.

> He asks, "Hey do you want to go
> to the hardware store?"
> I can tell he's trying
> to sound nonchalant
> but he's really excited to take me.

I tell him, "Of course I do!"

He's been wanting to build
a new bookshelf to fit in Chris's and my room.

I know it sounds sad
that I don't know what to say to Dad
sitting next to him in the car.

I know it's not his fault he has to work a lot
but sometimes
in my head
I blame him
for not being around.

For me feeling
so distant from him.

I wonder if,
on his long truck drives,
he thinks about
Chris and me.

I'm sure he does
but what does he think about?

I say, "Dad, I'm really sorry
about the car,"
but I can't stop thinking
about the last time
we rode together
on the way to say goodbye
to you, Lars.

>He looks at me. "Oh Claire,
>I'm just happy you're all right.
>Are you still upset about that?"

I almost start to cry.
It's both that I'm still upset
and just feeling sad about
how long it's been
since I really talked to Dad.

He looks like he has no idea
what to do.

He pulls over
and hugs me.

> He asks, "What's wrong? We're fine.
> Everything is fine."

"I just try so hard.
I just don't want to add
to everything you and Mom
have to do already.
I had a car and I ruined it,"
I say without being able
to stop myself.

> Dad looks at me, "Hey. Hey, I'm sorry.
> I know we put a lot of pressure on you
> to do well and you are. You're doing great.
> I'm sorry your mom and I made you feel like this.
> We all make mistakes.
> Don't worry about the car, really."

I cry more
but it's more of a "relief" cry now.
I didn't realize how much I needed to hear him say that.

I don't feel totally better but I do feel like
I'm finally feeling less guilty about you, Lars.

AT THE HARDWARE STORE

Dad gets the wood he needs
and he tells me his ideas
for building a bookshelf.
        "I want one
        you can put all your books
        and knickknacks
        and stuff on.
        Something you and Chris
        don't have to share."

"Knickknacks?" I ask, teasing.
"You mean my sculptures
and my stuffed animals?"

        "Knickknacks—those are
        knickknacks—you're looking at me
        like I sound old," he says.

"You do," I say.
"That's not bad though.
I do have some solid knickknacks."

Before checking out,
we pick out the same lollipops he used to buy me
when I was little
and I'd come to the hardware store with him.

They're big and round with swirls of color.

        Dad tells me, "You know,
        I'm excited to go to the fair as a family.
        It's been so long since
        I've been off for something like this."

COUNTDOWN: 1 DAY

And it's ten p.m. and Chris and I want to cry
but are too tired to cry.

We've taken a break from stressing
and are just laying on the floor of our room.

We pass the question back and forth
How do we tell our parents?   How do we tell our
parents?

In between, Chris texts the boy he likes.
FINALLY   he tells me, "His name is Jesse."

Chris makes me swear
to never tell his name to anyone

because he's not out yet and might not
want to be while he's in high school.

We're not sure
if, when we get to the fair,

we'll be able to just tell them.

> Chris says, "I just don't know
> if I can say 'Hi Mom and Dad I'm gay.'
> Like I'll freeze up!"

That's when I know what to do.

IN THIS TOGETHER

"What if I tell them you're gay," I say.
"Like, I could say, Chris wants you to know
that he's gay."

> "And I tell them you're bi," Chris says.

"Are you like comfortable with that?"
I ask.

"That sounds so much easier honestly," Chris says.
"But also kind of weird . . ."

"I think it's cute honestly."

"I want to write something more though
like a mini speech."

"Haha a speech about me?"

"Yeah kind of maybe more like a poem."

I hug Chris.

There are so many times
I wish I had my own room again

but if I wouldn't have had to be so close with Chris,
we might not have ever come out to each other.

I feel lucky that no matter what,
at least my brother will stick by me.

NIGHTMARE

We are all at the fair. The air smells like sweet funnel cakes and
candied apples. Carnival music swirls louder and louder. It slows
down and speeds up. I am walking toward my family: Dad, Mom,
and Chris. Their mouths are moving but no words are coming
out. The sky fills with fireworks. I am telling them I can't hear
them. They are putting their hands over their eyes and turning
their backs to me. I run around the fair and every single person is
looking away from me—it's like I'm not there. I find Sophia and
she's standing with Pen. I beg them to look at me but they are
still as statues. I scream and

next thing I know,
I'm sitting up in my bed.

Chris is still asleep.
I'm beading with sweat.

I stand up and lay down
on the carpet.

I wish I wasn't
so scared.

COUNTDOWN: TODAY

When I was little, on mornings when Dad was home,
Mom would bring out the waffle iron and make
all kinds of waffles: blueberry, strawberry, chocolate chip,
and more.

The sweet smell would wake me up.
This morning, the smell slips into our room.
I wake up before Chris. He sleeps like a skydiver,

all sprawled out as if he's falling.
I wonder why Mom is making waffles today.
Maybe she's excited about the fair.

We haven't gone to the fair all together since probably
when I was in middle school. We used to go every year.
We live in this small space together
but I guess we really don't actually spend much time together.

The waffle smells remind me of the brunch
Sophia and I had with Lena and Marie.
I decide it's a good omen and

I get ready for today.

PRAYING

I don't usually pray. In fact, I'm generally opposed to praying.
It makes me feel too much like God is watching me (weird).

Sometimes, Mom will hear a family member
or neighbor is sick and she'll say, "Pray for them."

I always wondered what that was supposed to do.
I've never seen someone get better or become healed from
praying.

Today, I think I understand. I want to pray that
everything will turn out all right tonight. I want to pray because

I don't know what else to do. I tell God I am sorry
I never try to talk to him. I tell God I want to believe he loves

queer people like my brother and me and that he wants
us to be loved and supported. I know this isn't how it always is.

I tell God I know he has to love queer people. I decide
my God, whoever he or she or they is, my God loves queer
people

and I'm going to pray to them that no matter what happens
I will get through—that my brother and I will be able to

love who we love
and not feel scared.

GIRLFRIEND

"Girlfriend" is a tricky word because
it can mean "best friends"
or "friends that are girls"
or that you're dating a girl.

Why isn't the word "boyfriends"
like that?

>	My mom says over breakfast,
>	"Have you seen any
>	of your girlfriends lately?
>	Are any of you meeting up
>	at the fair?"

I'm instantly scared she knows everything.

Then I remember you can use "girlfriend"
to just mean "friends."

I say, "I'm probably meeting up with Sophia."

> Mom says, "It's nice you two have been
> friends so long.
> I'm glad you're working things out.
> You'd said you had a little tiff."

"FRIENDS SO LONG"

I check my phone.
Hoping Sophia has texted me
so I don't have to text her first.

SOPHIA: Do you still want to meet up before we go?

ME: Sure, like when?

It's so early. Does she want to meet now?
I hope not, I'm still a nervous mess.

SOPHIA: What about five?

ME: Great!

That's perfect, it's about an hour before
my parents are coming.

What am I going to do with myself
all day?

> Mom says, "Hello?"

Which means "put your phone away."
I say, "Sorry, just figuring out plans
for tonight."

> Mom asks, "Chris, are you bringing anyone?"

Chris shrugs.

We share a knowing look.

He wants to meet up with his crush tonight
but isn't sure if Jesse will decide to come.

I hope Jesse comes. I know it's hard
but the fair is so special.

BRIEF INSTANCES OF MAGIC

When we were little,
Chris and I didn't miss a year at the fair for anything.

I remember taking his hand
and leading him toward the whirling lights of rides.

Sitting next to each other on the Ferris wheel
together, we'd hope to be stopped at the top

to see the town spread out around us.
Us, above everything.

I believed the carnival lights
and music and clinking metal rides

had to be magic.
I thought the fair was full of ghosts.

I used to imagine that
at the fair there might be no way of telling

a living person from a spirit.
I think maybe I watched too much Syfy channel

or maybe I was looking for somewhere
magic might exist. I think there's something rare

about an occasion that only comes once a year.
I know it sounds naïve or ridiculous

but I trust the energy of the fair
to protect us.

I spend the early afternoon
rehearsing in my head what I will tell my parents

about my brother. I can tell Chris is
doing the same. I wish the clock would
move a little faster.
I wonder if Lena ever felt like this

when she came out.
I want to go visit her to ask for more advice

but I know I need to live this myself.
She's already helped me so much.

CANDY APPLES

I decide to get to the fair before Sophia
to buy her a candy apple.

The last time we went together,
she kept looking for a candy apple

and I was looking for a caramel one.
We'd peer in the windows of

the little food carts.
We saw the bubbling fryers

and soft pretzels under heat lamps
but no apples.

It was the last night of the fair,
so they were all sold out. I hope

she remembers and doesn't think
it's weird of me to go buy her one.

CARAMEL APPLES

I pay for a wrist band: hot pink.
The familiar feeling on my skin
makes me wish I was ten again
and unaware of so much.

It's early, so the fair isn't very crowded yet.
I look around to see if I recognize anyone from school.
I'm bad at staying in touch
over the summer. I only usually hang out once or twice

with people other than Sophia.
I notice the apple stand so I figure I'll just start there.
There's only one person in line.
Long brown hair. Familiar long brown hair.

Her olive-green short shorts. Her pink converse.
It's Sophia! I'm disappointed she beat me
to getting a candy apple.
She turns around and sees me.
She's holding a caramel apple.

She looks startled to see me.
She jogs over to where I'm standing on the gravel fairway.
        "It was supposed to be a surprise!" she says,
        handing the apple to me.

"I was trying to get here early
to get you a candy one,
can I still buy one for you?"
I ask.

        "Aw you're so sweet," she says.
        She looks flustered,
        like she wants to say something.

My heart is beating so fast.
I feel like the whole carnival has blurred
into nothing and it's just me and Sophia standing there.

SOPHIA SAYS

"I guess I wanted to get you something
to say I'm sorry.

Things have been weird with us.
I feel like it's my fault but also just like
I'm also going to blame
the cisheteropatriarchy.

I got freaked out about what Pen said—
about you liking me because I was scared
about like a whole other coming out.

Part of the reason things didn't work with Theo is
I really don't think I like boys at all.

Well, that and like he was a controlling asshole.

I always felt like that was like the ultimate thing
especially like for a trans girl
was to like be with a straight guy.

To realize I only like girls is like scary.

It's like people are going to be shitty to me
for being trans AND for being a lesbian?

THEN it felt like extra scary
that the person I like
is my best friend.

I don't want
everything to change.

Not just us but school and life
and everything.

It all moves so fast.

I want to leave
this town but

at the same time,
I don't think
I've had enough time.

Am I making any sense???"

I TAKE A STEP FORWARD

So we're eye to eye.
She smells sweet
like she always does.
She smiles.
We're both crying now
and I kiss her.

KISSING SOPHIA

And for a few moments we aren't anywhere
we are just   Sophia and Claire
Claire and Sophia   nowhere else
as if we are each other's destinations.
Sophia keeps saying,   "I'm sorry I didn't say something
sooner."
I hold her   and I say,
"It doesn't matter."   We pull apart
looking at each other as the carnival comes back into focus.

WHERE ARE WE?

When we stop, we both seem to remember
where we are   at the same moment.

We take a half step   back from each other
and look around nervously.   Did anyone we know see us?

Oh gosh,
why did we have to kiss where everyone can see?

No. No, it's okay,   no one is really looking.
We're off to the side enough.   Our faces are flushed.
We share   a nervous laugh.

We say "I'm sorry"   at the same time
          and laugh again.

I ask if I can hold her hand   while we walk the fairgrounds.
          She smiles and agrees.

          Sophia says, "It's funny because people probably think
          we're just holding hands
          because we're best friends."

I kiss her shoulder and say,
"We are best friends.
I want to still be best friends."

I tell her,
"My parents are coming soon
and I'm nervous.
Like I told you,
we're going to come out
here at the fair."

          Sophia says,
          "No matter what
          I'll be here for you guys.
          Ugh, do you think
          I have to tell my parents
          I'm a lesbian?"

"You never 'have to' if you don't
want to," I say.

          "That's true," Sophia says.
          "Maybe I'll just let them figure it out."

ODE TO SOPHIA

I think odes might be best
when they're about something simple or specific
like a car
    or a vase
        or a cool night in July.

I don't think I will ever be able
to write a real ode about Sophia.

As we walk around the fair,
holding hands and talking,

I keep thinking
this is going to end
and she's going to say
she changed her mind.

She doesn't though.

The cool night wind blows through her hair.
The sunset is bruised-peach orange.

We talk about all the little moments
that made us realize we liked each other
more than just as friends. Sophia says
she knew she couldn't hide it anymore
after going out with Lena and Marie.

She says she imagined us as old ladies—
that meeting two old queer women
made her realize her feelings
were real and not just a phase
or a passing emotion.

TEXT MESSAGE

MOM: Hi there! We're heading over!

MOM: Chris is already there.

MOM: Where should we meet?

ME: Front gate?

MOM: Oh yeah duh. See you soon ☺

ME: I'll text Chris ☺

> What I love about texting is sometimes
> an emoji can make you sound fine
> when you're actually freaking out.

"WHAT CAN I DO TO HELP?"

Sophia keeps asking,
> "What can I do to help?"

I keep wishing
> there was something
>> she really *could* do.

"Can you fast-forward time?"
I ask.

> "I can try,"
>> she says.

We see Chris after
only a few moments
of looking for him.

The fair is small and he always has
his lime-green backpack.

He's with THE boy!
Maybe it's Jesse!

317

It HAS to be Jesse.

In that moment,
I'm so, so happy he's my brother
and we're in this together.

> "I'm gonna go,"
> Sophia says.
> "I want to meet up with some friends
> from Dunkin' and give you
> and your brother some space.
> You understand, right?"

I want to cling to her
and tell her to stay with me
but I know it would just
make things even more complicated
especially if my parents don't take it well.

"Have fun,"
I say.

> "See you soon," she says.
> "And call me if you need me."

REHEARSING

Me: "Mom, Dad, Chris likes boys. He's gay."

> Chris: "No, the other way around."

Me: "Mom, Dad, Chris is gay, he likes boys."

> Chris: "No, leave out the 'likes boys,'
> they should know what that means, right?"

Me: "I hope."

> Chris: "Mom, Dad, Claire is a lesbian."

Me: "No, no, no I'm bisexual."

Chris: "Sorry, I'm just nervous. Duh. I'm sorry."

Me: "Bi-erased by my own brother."

Chris: "They'll be here soon, let's try again.
Mom, Dad, Claire is bisexual which means
she likes both genders."

Me: "Bisexual people (and me) also like nonbinary people,
so say 'multiple genders.'"

Chris: "They are going to be so confused by that."

Me: "Ugh you're right."

Chris: "What about 'Claire likes boys and girls and any
other genders'?"

Me: "Sure, yes that's good!"

Chris: "Mom, Dad . . ."

I pinch Chris's arm.

I see Mom and Dad coming.

They're beaming as they buy tickets.

Mom gives us a little wave and a soft smile.

Haven't seen them this genuinely happy in a while.

I have this thought:

I feel like guilty for possibly ruining it.

A FAMILY

As we stand together and look out at the fair,
Mom asks, "So what are we doing first?"

I feel nervous.
I feel almost the same way I feel when
I hang out with someone new.

Why do I feel like this
around them? My own family.

I'm realizing it's hard to feel
like a family sometimes
even when your apartment is small
and you only live a few feet from each other.

I'm hit with the wave of missing them.
I'm remembering all the summers
Chris and I came
to the fair with our parents.

I'm remembering
        watching the fireworks from my dad's lap.
I'm remembering
        Mom carrying me to the car and
                the sweet rosewater smell of her hair.

Dad is always working. Mom is always working.
Chris and I are always   buried in homework
or working
                            or walking outside
to try to find
                            a fragment of ourselves

        in this tiny town.
        Everything is so small.

I'm realizing it is hard to feel like a family
when there is always so much to be done,
and even harder when your identity

makes you want to pull further away.

I want to cry just thinking about this
but I don't. I hold it together.

I want to get food first. It sounds like
an easy way to start talking.

Chris says, "We should split a funnel cake."

Mom asks, "Before dinner?"
Dad says, "AS dinner!"

ANOTHER FAMILY

I wish Lena could be with us.
I know that's silly. I know I only met her this summer
but she feels like my family too.

I know she can't fix everything. It's just
comforting to know there are queer people
of all different ages and in all different places.

I think of brunch together and I remember
that this is also not the last night of my life.
There will be a next week

and a next month and a next year
and hopefully maybe another brunch
all together.

HOW TO EAT FUNNEL CAKE

First, the powdered sugar.
Chris and I both
take a shaker and dust the golden-fried dough.

Mom says, "That's enough!"

Dad says, "No more!"

We get white sugar all over our fingers.
Chris licks the dust off his fingers
and I call him gross, wiping mine off
with a flimsy brown-paper napkin.

Chris tears off the first piece,
dough still hot from the fryer. He breathes steam
from his mouth and we all laugh.

Dad takes a huge chunk and folds it all
into his mouth.

Mom says, "Don't eat it all, I want some."

She takes a small piece and takes an even smaller bite.
I do the same as her.

"You can't keep up," Chris says.

He takes a Dad-sized piece
and so, I take a bigger one too.

We are laughing and the sugar is
going everywhere.

"We should have gotten two," Mom says.

"One for us and one for them," I say.

Mom smiles and we all wipe our mouths
with brown-paper napkins.

My fingers are still sticky.

Mom says, "We definitely should have gotten dinner first."

Dad says, "At the fair we eat backward."

Across the fair is a sit-down eating area
with actual meals. We walk there.

Dad talks about getting more sleep
than he's gotten in months
and Mom talks about dyeing someone's hair orange today
and Chris and I look at each other,

knowing it's time for us to tell them.

NEVER A RIGHT TIME

The time feels right
but also,
the time feels wrong.
Maybe it's because
coming out isn't something
I think we should have to do at all.
No matter where we decided
to do it, it feels so random
to just be like, "Hey Mom and Dad,
my brother is gay!"

COMING-OUT STORIES

I can't help but think about Lena
and how different it must have been
for her to be out or to come out.

I wonder where the phrase
"coming out" even came from
and I wish stories about queer people

weren't always about coming out.
But, maybe coming out isn't always about
coming out. I know that sounds crazy

but hear me out. It's a moment where
you get to mark something—declare this part
of yourself. The world moves so fast,

it's hard to find moments where you feel
like your life is real—like the world is something
you can touch. Coming out is like saying,

"I am a person." Maybe all stories
are coming-out stories. Sometimes, Mom will tell us about
when she decided she wanted to become a hairdresser.

Her parents were disappointed. They'd wanted her
to try to go to community college. They wanted her to
"go get more for herself than them." The first time she told us,

I didn't know what that meant. Mom loved her job.
What more did anyone want? So maybe coming out
is also about shaking expectations other people put on you

by saying, "This is who I am no matter
what other people might expect of me."

CHRIS STARTS

"Can I talk about something important?"

They both say,
"Yeah—yeah of course."

"I know, I know. I just wanted to ask first."

Sound of a carnival ride clinking   around and
around.
Sound of   a child laughing.   A
balloon popping at a game booth.
The ding of a bell.

"You have to promise to listen and not say anything till I'm
done,"
Chris says.

"I know, of course you will.
It's just important and it's not about me."

"All right, so Claire.
She's the best sister in the world,
which is yuck, super cheesy but it's true."

"She wants to tell you something but I'm going to tell you
because she's too scared to say it
and we decided it would be easier this way."

"Claire is bisexual, which means she likes
any gender. So, she likes girls and boys
and people who are both or neither.
She wanted me to tell you here."

Sound of the trash can lid opening   and closing.
Rustling tree branches.   A fizzle of soda.

I SAY

"And I want to tell you something about Chris."

I see a photo album inside my head,
which is funny because
the only photo albums we have
are of Chris and me as babies.

I see all the moments of us when we were little.
We draw with sidewalk chalk. We lay in the shade of trees.
We drip sugary popsicle syrup down our forearms.

I become aware of the texture of the picnic table
and cool prickling breeze.

"Chris is gay. He likes guys."

"He has known this for a while
and he wanted me to tell you."

"I'm proud of him
and you should be too.
I'm lucky to be his sister."

MOM AND DAD

Mom and Dad
don't say anything
for such a long time.

The sounds of the fair around us seem to swell
louder and louder.

Am I breathing?

I inhale slowly and exhale slowly, trying to just stay present.

    Mom starts crying
  and Mom never cries so we don't know
      what to do
          and Dad is patting her back
        and at first I can't hear what she's saying
    through her crying

I'm panicking,
        what does this mean?

Dad has his arm around her,
            what is happening?

I think of packing up all my belongings
                and leaving with Chris.

        Where would we go?

What would we do?
            What should we do?

Can we take it back?

"DID YOU THINK I WOULDN'T LOVE YOU?"

    Mom says,
    and Dad is saying, "No, no, honey. It's okay."

and I'm crying and saying,
"No! No!
I didn't think that—"

    and Chris is saying,
    "Mom no—we were just scared."
        Everyone but Chris is crying and Mom
    is dabbing her eyes with the gritty brown napkins
    and she keeps saying,
        "I'm sorry.
            God, I'm sorry."

Mom says,
"I can't believe I made you feel like that."

ODE TO MOM AND DAD

I've tried to write poems for Mom and Dad
on Mother's Day and Father's Day and

on their birthdays
but they never feel good enough.

Writing those poems always makes me feel younger—
like I'm ten years old again. Like I'm small

and looking up at them—like Dad is going to pick me up
and carry me to bed or like Mom is

going to ask to give me a fishtail braid for church.
I don't want to be younger but I miss how easy it seemed

before I started to understand
that Mom and Dad are just people too.

They aren't perfect (ha! what a terrible ode this is) but they are
trying. Sometimes trying isn't always enough.

I think sometimes people try in the wrong directions
or confusing directions but I look at them

and I know they love us and that
none of what it means to be a family is easy.

I look at Dad's coarse hands
and Mom's pink fingernails.

I look at my own hands
and see the creases of their hands in my own.

IMPERFECT /

Is there a perfect thing someone could say
when you come out to them?

I guess maybe it would be nice
if they just said, "We support you."

Or maybe,
"We're proud of you."

But I know reactions are sometimes
a little messier than that.

> Dad blinks and says,
> "That makes sense."

Which I think is hilarious
but when I laugh,
Chris doesn't.

He looks hurt and I feel bad
for thinking it was funny.

It was like Dad was saying,
"Yes, you two seem weird,"
which isn't necessarily a bad thing.

We are unique
and a little weird sometimes
but that's not because we're queer.

I guess maybe that hurts Chris.

> Mom says, "Yes, yes I suppose it does."
> She smiles weakly as if to tell us

> she's happy or at least not upset.

They don't say anything else

for a long awkward pause.

/ PERFECT

> "That's interesting,"
> Mom adds.

She's trying to keep the mood light

as neither Chris or I
can think of anything to say.

> "It's not, actually, it's just who I am—
> it's no big deal.
> Nothing changes about me,"
> Chris says.

Which IS interesting to me because
I do feel like something
has been changing about me.

I don't know if I will ever
feel the same way about being queer
as he does. Which is okay.

> Mom continues,
> "Of course, Chris, we love you.
> We love you no matter what.
> I do worry but—but we can talk
> about that later."

Chris sighs.
I don't know what she's
"worried" about but
it will probably be
some kind of microaggression.

They did almost get there,
it just took a second.

Dad is still speechless, which worries me,
but when isn't he speechless?

MOM SAYS, "CAN I ASK A QUESTION?"

Chris and I look at each other.
We're just thankful it's not silent.

Awkward silence is almost always worse
than an awkward conversation.

I'm already feeling a little bit lighter
like I could just float and hover right above the fair—

look down at all the lights and my small town around us.
I feel less scared for the first time since the summer started.

"Sure!" Chris and I both say.

"The questions is more for you," Mom says, looking at me.
"Is this why you wanted
to cut your hair?" she asks.

We both laugh this time.

ODE TO SHORT HAIR IN JULY

Cool breeze on the back of my neck.
No hair in my face.
A lifting feeling.
I've been new
over and over this summer.

I've been new.
A lifting feeling.
No hair in my face
over and over this summer.
Cool breeze on the back of my neck.

A lifting feeling
over and over this summer.
No hair in my face.
Cool breeze on the back of my neck.
I've been new.

LOOKING QUEER

I want to look queer but it feels uncomfortable
when Mom points it out.

It feels like she's pointing out
my difference. Sometimes people say "lesbian"

like it's a bad thing
without thinking about it.

"Well, I am queer but a haircut doesn't make someone queer,"
I say. I'm proud of myself

for saying how I feel. I always try
to make Mom happy but that means

for a long time, she never knew
how I actually felt.

She apologizes profusely. She says,
        "I'm an idiot. I'm new at this."

And I understand. I wonder if
we'll keep talking about this or if

they're both just going to
never bring it up again.

We finish eating. We walk down the line
of carnival games.

I want to win a big, stupid stuffed animal
for Sophia.

AWKWARD / OKAY

It does feel weird.
Our parents are still a little stunned
and Chris and I can tell because
they hardly say anything

the rest of the night.
What they do say, though,
is what matters.

> Mom says, "You know I love you.
> You know I love you."

> > Dad says, "This is the best night
> > of the summer"

> > and

> > "I need to take off more."

I hug Chris every other minute
because I can't say,
"We're okay! It's all okay,"
in front of our parents.

A TINY STUFFED ELEPHANT

We play almost all the games on the fairway.
I throw darts. Chris tries and fails at the basketball game.
We all try and fail to win a goldfish. Eventually,
Dad asks if we can just buy one and the man at the stand looks
both ways
and agrees. Mom wants to name the fish "Lucky"
to counteract our luck at the games. None of us are winning.
Dad is on goldfish duty. He holds the fish gently with both hands.
The archery game has the biggest prizes. I try again and again
with no luck. It doesn't seem like I'll be winning Sophia anything
tonight.
Then, we try this silly game where you pick ducks up
from a pool of water and read the number written on the bottom.
I pick a duck up and get to pick a small prize. There are little
boxes of candy
and kazoos but I want to pick the tiny stuffed elephant.
It has a little blue bow and is only the size of my palm.
Perfect, it's perfect.

FIREWORKS I

Right before the fireworks, everyone starts to congregate
in the field on the far side of the fairgrounds.

I text Sophia to try to find her.
I feel bad

we haven't hung out much tonight.
I know she'll understand but I still miss her.

ME: I want to see the fireworks with you
ME: I miss youuuuuuu

SOPHIA: I miss you too lol
SOPHIA: And uhhh duh! I've been waiting for you!

How can I miss her when I just saw her?
I wonder if what I mean by "miss" is more like

I feel like a part of me is missing without Sophia.
There's no hope for me. I'm so in love with her.

Walking with my family, I hear "Claire!!!"
and I turn to see her. She waves and jogs over to meet us.

She gives me a look as if to ask, "How did it go?"
I nod and smile. She comes to sit with us.

Mom and Dad look at us a little too long.
I know what they're wondering.

I'm sure I'll have to talk to them later but right now,
I don't care. I'm just happy to be with Sophia.

We talk about all the past years at the fair
and the old rides and the new rides.

I want to hold her hand. She smiles
and takes mine carefully. I hold her hand tight.

FIREWORKS II

I'm wondering if Jesse will join us too. I see the boy across the
field with some of Chris's other friends. They wave to Chris and
Chris waves back. I try to make a face at Chris to tell him to go
over and hang out with them. Chris shakes his head. At first, I
think it's because he's scared Mom and Dad will see him with
Jesse, then

> Chris says, "I just want to stay with you guys. I have all
> summer to be with my friends." I don't know if I'd say
> something like that when I was fourteen. I just wanted to
> get away from everyone. Half the time I still do. I think
> about how different Chris and I are even as siblings—even
> as siblings who share the same tiny bedroom—even as
> queer siblings who came out on the same night together.

FIREWORKS III

There is
this moment of quiet
right before the first firework leaps into the air.

The sound of a night bug chorus
fills the field.
Far off,

we see people standing
with long glowing flares
to light the fireworks.

I put my arm around Sophia
and I am not scared anymore
of loving her.

Everyone is looking up
in anticipation.
Mom and Dad are holding each other too

and Chris is sitting with his knees
tucked into his chest.
I love all of them, I think,

and then there comes
the soft sound of the firework
climbing into the sky.

FIREWORKS IV

Scattering of light:
    red, orange, yellow,
        maroon, pink, mauve, green,
            blue, blue, blue.

I find rainbows
    in between the fireworks.
        I find us and I find
            a brilliant future.

Blooming fragments
    a fiery carnation
        a glowing rose
            an illuminated hydrangea.

I find her hand in mine
    and I find my family
        and I find my tiny town
            glistening with light.

ODE TO EXHAUSTION

When we get home after the carnival,
we take off our shoes by the door. We talk

in mumbles and tired words.
Dad tries to ruffle my hair and misses

poking me in the forehead
and we laugh. Mom kisses my head.

Chris and I zombie-walk
into our bedroom and I wonder if

we would have come out to each other
if we hadn't moved into this smaller place.

I don't believe things always happen
for a reason, but I'm happy

we found each other and
found our family again.

I say, "Chris, I love you."
      Chris says, "I love you too."

We turn off the lights.

*

BRUNCH

July felt so long
but also so, so short.

I can't believe it's already August.

Tuesdays we always get brunch
with Marie and Lena. Today, we all order
French toast and Sophia tells Marie and Lena

about watching the fireworks with me.
Lena tells a story
about going to a carnival

with one of her first girlfriends—
how they were scared to hold each other's hands
but embraced in the dark
by the glow of fireworks.

I think about how brunch is kind of like
the opposite of fireworks in the dark.

The sun is blaring and bright
out the diner window. I wonder
what we look like to other people at the diner.

After we're done, Marie asks
if I want to try driving her car
to take Lena back home.

Sophia nudges me and tells me
she knows I've been missing driving.
I adjust the seat and the mirrors

and pull off onto the road.
The wind runs through
our hair.

AUTHOR'S NOTE

When writing this book, I set out to explore what it would have been like if I were more out in high school as a bisexual girl. I didn't understand myself as a nonbinary person until I was in college, so I experienced high school as a queer girl. This is not how all trans people would talk about their pre-transition selves, but it's how I understand mine. I say "more out" because I knew I was bisexual probably since seventh grade, but I had a hard time telling people. Really, I had a hard time telling myself. Then, when I did come out, I was often met with biphobia and homophobia. People would tell me that I was bisexual "for attention." Then, I faced similar struggles most queer girls do like, in the girl's locker room, I remember walking in one day to see everyone had moved their lockers away from me. Someone had started I rumor I watched people while they changed just because I'd come out to a few people as bi.

It wasn't all hard though. I do think I connected deeply with other queer girls as I grew up and now, as a nonbinary person, I have such a great community of queer folks around me. I'm so glad to be bisexual, queer, and trans.

In many ways, this book is a love letter to the messy but wonderful bisexual girl I was. I hope Claire can give us a little more permission to embrace ourselves and take a chance on love (as cliché as that sounds). I've definitely experienced being in love with a close friend. I hope maybe Claire and Sophia's story can open us up to talk about our feelings. Even if Sophia didn't also love Claire back like she does in the story, I think they could have still grown from her sharing that. Talking openly about how we feel in a respectful and kind way is important for any kind of relationship.

Even now there's a lot of bisexual erasure and biphobia that goes on in the LGBTQIA+ community. I hope we can move toward a time where we celebrate our unique queerness and vibrant, beautiful love.

I have often heard friends or people online wishing they had more of a connection with queer older adults. I think I'm guilty of ageism in the sense that I don't often reach out to people much older than myself to learn about their experiences. I think this is especially important as queer people. We have so much to learn from one another and we owe so much to previous generations of LGBTQIA+ people. I wrote Marie and Lena imagining what solidarity and love could look like for queers across ages. We need each other so much. I hope we can work toward celebrating and honoring one another.

ACKNOWLEDGMENTS

I first want to thank my editor, Trisha de Guzman. I don't think this story would have taken shape in the way it has without your wonderfully inviting questions and guidance. You helped open up Claire's and Sophia's personalities, so they could flourish. Also, a huge thanks to my agent, Jordan Hamessley, for helping me share this book. So thankful for all your support, insight, and enthusiasm for my poetry.

I'm grateful to all my wonderful bisexual and/or queer friends who've always made me feel proud to be bi and queer, especially Jey, Solana, Ben, Joe, Paige, Gabby, Rain, Morty, Ryan, Lisa, and Benny. And, lots of love to my partner, Saturn.

A special thanks goes to my queer elders. I hope we can build a future where there are more spaces where we can learn from each other. Books like this can exist because of the work LGBTQIA+ leaders have done.